SHOOT ME, JESUS

Tales of the Old & New Southwest

A Novel in Short Stories

Brian Allan Skinner

Nighthawk Press

TAOS, NEW MEXICO

Nighthawk Press
PO Box 1222
Taos, New Mexico 87571
www.nighthawkpress.com

Cover art: "Quod Sum" © 2018 by Brian Allan Skinner
All interior illustrations © 2018 by Brian Allan Skinner
www.brianskinner.net

Publisher's Note: This is a work of fiction. Names, characters, places, and incidents are a product of the author's imagination. Locales and public names are sometimes used for atmospheric purposes. Any resemblance to actual people, living or dead, or to businesses, companies, events, institutions, or locales is completely coincidental

Shoot Me, Jesus/ Brian Allan Skinner – 1st edition
ISBN 978-0-9986807-4-3
Library of Congress Control Number: 2018948015

CONTENTS

Acknowledgments

If I were to thank all those who provided inspiration for these tales, the list would have to include nearly everyone I ever met, not leaving out a few random passersby.

Most of the help I received in turning these tales into polished stories came from other writers, in particular, Jane Lawless and Syed Afzal Haider from our Monadnock Fiction Workshops days in Chicago. I remain in close touch with both Jane and Syed.

For their patient ears and helpful suggestions, I thank David Breitkopf and David L. Hamsley from my years of living and working in New York City.

Now that I am a Taoseño, I want to express my gratitude to Jan Smith, Rose Gordon, Dianne Vona, and Sandra Richardson whose peerless critiques at SOMOS, the Society of the Muse of the Southwest, helped me whip this latest batch of stories into shape.

I do not want to leave out the members of the No Coast Writers here in Taos: Susan Mihalic, Lauren Bjorkman, Brian Tacang, Martha Grossman, Eileen Wiard, Susan Washburn, Mary-George Eggborn, and Janet Majerus.

I'd be in double trouble if I failed to mention my long-suffering spouse, Mary Skinner, and partner Anthony Fountain, who often read first drafts of earlier collections and dealt with the weather of my temperament.

Lastly, but first in my mind, I thank my mother, Elaine, who read to me ceaselessly when I was a child, and to my father, George, who worked overtime at a job he didn't like to afford sending me to a good school. Though both are dead, they live on in me and in my stories.

Brian Allan Skinner

Author's Note

I call the collection of tales in **Shoot Me, Jesus** a "novel in short stories." Other terms for a group of related stories are "short story cycle" and "linked stories." Each of these concepts conveys a bit of what I am up to with this anthology.

Novels I conceive of as being primarily plot-driven and having all the room in the world—or the writer's imagination— for excessive detail, rambling asides, and dead ends. This is not to say that I don't like novels, but the short story is a different sort of literary critter, leaner and meaner. As a writer, I find short stories more challenging.

The stories here move forward and backward in time much in the manner of flashbacks and foreshadowing in a novel, though the plots are always character-driven. It is their realizations, insights, and inner changes that move my tales along.

While my characters retain their essences from story to story, the details of their lives, from their occupations to their sexual proclivities, change with each story. Their identities are malleable, yet who they are remains consistent. They develop by a process of accretion, a slow accumulation of personality traits.

After the first story, which I had no idea would lead to a collection of stories, I wondered how things might have turned out for the protagonist if he liked men instead of women, or was poor rather than comfortable. A mere ten seconds can mean the difference between life and death. The smallest event can have enormous repercussions down the road, a kind of "butterfly effect" on a human life. I wanted to explore those concepts in short fiction.

While I conceived of each of these stories as a stand-alone tale that can be read in any order, the order in which I have presented them is meant to help the reader come to a realization of who my characters are and what they are about.

Though I do not recall the source, a fellow author said that each writer has a stable of six distinct characters and the others are variations on one of those six themes. I also make use of that idea in this collection.

I hope you enjoy the tales of *Shoot Me, Jesus*, what writer Jane Lawless called "erotic magic realism with a Southwestern spiciness." I certainly had a good deal of fun writing them.

Brian Allan Skinner

A GHOST IN THE ATTIC

The frost ferns creep imperceptibly across the window panes. From my bed, dressed in all the clothes I own, I shiver beneath the wool army blanket my father left me. It is full of holes. The cold air of the attic makes my breath steam. I watch the moon rise behind the silvery vegetation. It is nearly full—two more nights. A dog howls from miles away.

My bed is an old mattress I dragged to the chimney wall. It is slightly warmer there, the bricks absorbing the last of the heat before it rises into the cloudless night sky. The attic is not a room I rent, but one I appropriated. After climbing up a trellis and onto the gable next door, I lifted myself to the sill and lowered myself through the attic window.

I've learned everyone's habits in the neighborhood so I won't be surprised or give a shock to anyone else, resulting in the police being called. I don't like snooping on people, but I am bored. It's like watching television is for some people: a way to while away long hours.

Despite my care to be quiet, removing my boots at the windowsill, the boy in the tiny bedroom on the floor beneath me reported ghosts. No one believed him, of course. I make sure the attic trapdoor remains secured with a board across it from the inside. Children are as clever as you expect them not to be. I have not forgotten how to be a child.

Tonight, the boy has been sent to bed early. I heard his father yelling at him and something shattered. I roll to the edge of the mattress and remove the floorboard just above the ceiling fixture of his room where a chunk of plaster is missing. I feel the warmth stream through the hole, the moisture condensing into a cloud around my head.

The boy lights an old railroad lantern with a match and sets it on the table beside his bed. Next to the lantern, in a small wooden box, are his collection of quarters, which he lays out and counts in piles of four. Nearly ten bucks. Then he takes out a braided leather bracelet and, with the aid of his right hand and teeth, winds it around his left wrist and knots it. He climbs beneath the covers in his longjohns and flannel shirt. I know it is not polite to spy on others, but the boy reminds me of someone. He dims the lantern way down, but does not extinguish the flame.

I watch him bury his face in his pillow and sob, his head emerging now and then to gulp in air. He's in the vicinity of twelve years old, not too old for a boy to cry his heart out. In time he settles down and turns onto his back. The olive-drab army blanket on his bed is intact and tightly tucked in.

I replace the floorboard and roll over to the chimney. Pulling the blanket over my head, I breathe through one of its ragged holes. Trying to remember of whom the boy makes me think, I return to scenes of sixth grade that still haunt me. Before tumbling off to sleep, I recall part of a poem from that time, I don't remember by whom.

> A keening
> not the wind,
> reaching shadows
> not the trees,
> a shiver
> not from cold.
>
> Running
> does not avail,
> nor screaming
> summon help.
>
> So I bow
> to accept my fate.

When my nocturnal rounds among restaurant garbage cans do not provide me enough to eat, I steal to the kitchen pantry downstairs. I do not attempt this unless famished, and only when I have seen or heard every member of the household leave for the day. I abscond with the crust of bread or wedge of cheese that might not be missed. My stomach flutters from the moment I remove the plank of wood securing the attic trapdoor until I have returned upstairs and replaced it.

The family dog, a wiry-haired mutt named Argus, pays me no mind, though our first encounter saw us running from each other as fast as six legs could carry us. Watchdog is not one of his talents. Now, the bribery of a treat from the pantry ensures his silence. And if he is left in the yard when I descend from the neighbor's trellis at night, he keeps it zipped even without a dog biscuit. As a boy, I'd always longed for a loyal pal like Argus.

I save half my bread for later so that my rumbling stomach doesn't keep me awake. I stash it beneath the loose floorboard so I don't have to think about it. Instead I contemplate making my presence known to the boy. I could be the ghost he heard in the attic, a congenial spirit in whom he can confide, pouring out his heart to someone who only listens, who offers advice only when asked, a grown-up—albeit deceased—he could trust.

Each morning the boy's father or, sometimes, his mother calls him downstairs. The boy's name is Tony. It will help knowing his name. I watch from the attic window on the street side as he leaves for school and comes home again. I wait for him to go up to his room after supper.

Tony turns in immediately and reads for a while, cowled beneath his blanket. From my vantage I cannot read the title, but the pages look like poetry. Poor kid.

When he has gone through his evening ritual of counting quarters and putting on the leather bracelet, I call down to him through the opening.

"Fear not," I say, lowering my voice in an attempt to sound

spooky but not frightening. "I am a friendly spirit."

He bolts upright in bed and turns up the kerosene lantern. He dashes for the doorway.

Before he screams, or calls downstairs, I rush to add, "I can tell you things, Tony."

"You mean, like secrets?" the boy asks, pausing, but inching toward the stairs.

"Maybe," I reply in a cloud of breath. I think of the affair his father is having with Adele down the street, Tuesdays and Thursdays during the lunch hour. But he would not understand.

"Name one," Tony insists.

I have to think of the right one, a small one, but one he can verify.

"It is Adám next door who took your flashlight. He hid it beneath his back step."

"I knew it," he says, rather loudly.

His father hollers for him to pipe down and go to sleep. If Tony wants heat from downstairs, he must keep his door open. If he wants privacy and closes it, he must shiver.

"That's all for tonight," I tell Tony.

He dims his railway lantern, though much less than usual. I return to my bed, now cold, and watch Orion rise beyond the window frame. I doze off trying to remember at what age I stopped believing in ghosts.

———◦———

Life grows easier with the arrival of spring, but the attic turns hot during the day. I open the windows at either end of the peak just a crack from the top. I can't imagine how I will endure summer.

There are two leaks when it rains. The noise on the tin roof is deafening. Lightning strikes terrifyingly close, rumbling the rafters. I collect rainwater when the gutter overflows and store it in milk jugs. I have to lean far out the window. When there's enough water, I use it to wash myself. If I need to pee, I go into an empty water jug, taking it to the downstairs toilet when it's full. The other business I do in an empty lot overgrown with sagebrush and chamisa. I don't eat much, so I don't go much.

I hear Tony opening and shutting the drawers of a small chest, frantically searching for something from the sound of it. He switches on his desk lamp and mutters to himself about being stupid. I decide he may want to talk.

"I don't think you're especially stupid, Tony. No more than anyone else."

"Thanks."

"Should I not tell you the truth?"

"No, you're right," he admits. "I can't find my leather bracelet. I can't lose it. A boy at school gave it to me. We're friends."

I realize it's a long shot, but I tell him to check under the bed. I can't afford to be wrong.

He turns the lamp up and crawls beneath the bed, emerging with his leather wrist band.

"You're a genius!" he declares.

"No, just a genie."

Tony's father hollers upstairs for him to get his "ass in bed" or he can expect another whipping. The boy switches off the desk lamp.

"Another?" I ask Tony in a whisper.

"Later," he says, crawling into bed and turning down the lantern on his bed table.

I go back to my mattress, now sitting beneath the wide-open window not visible from the street. I have trouble falling asleep. My memory smarts from the whippings I received from my father with his leather belt. A streetcar conductor, he hung his heavy coin changer from it. At other times, if he bypassed the tavern on his way home, I might merit a quarter. I never knew which one of him was going to walk through the door. Neither did my mother.

Nearly asleep, I am jolted awake by the memory of a piece of braided leather I carried with me for years. It was at the bottom of the knapsack someone stole from me at the train depot in Mewoo, Kansas. At last I fall asleep to the rhythmic swaying of the train and the clacking of the tracks beneath me. I wonder where I will awaken.

———◦◦———

Tony comes home from school in the company of another lanky boy. They jostle at the front gate and push each other onto the lawn, wrestling in the wet grass. I want to warn Tony that he'll be punished for getting his clothes wet and dirty, but I keep quiet. Ghosts appear only under cover of dark.

Tony and his buddy race up the walkway. The front door slams and a herd of feet rushes up the steps to his room. I remove the floorboard.

The boys are both dressed in worn Levi's, T-shirt, and gym shoes. They sit at the edge of the bed, speaking softly. I dare not lean down closer.

Tony takes his braided leather bracelet from the wooden box and hands it to his friend.

"You put it on me this time, Mitch," he says. "I'll never take it off."

The boy ties it around Tony's wrist. They poke each other and laugh. Mitch pushes his buddy backwards onto the bed. Each struggles half-heartedly for the upper hand. They collapse, giggling, into each other's arms. They entwine their blue-jeaned legs and kiss each other frantically on the lips. I replace the floorboard.

Poor child, I think. *You'll have a hard life. But everyone has a hard life. A much harder life, then.*

I feel the cool streak of an unexpected tear roll down my cheek. Or maybe it is just a drop of sweat. I hope it will rain and cool down soon. It is too hot to sleep.

———◦◦———

Tony slams his door and calls up to me. Needing a proper ghostly name, I told him I used to be called Sixtus van Thorson III in life, making it up on the spot. He calls me Mr. Six. It is his last day of grade school. He is thirteen. I expect him to be in good spirits. I like to think he looks forward to our talks.

"Help me," he wails. "I'm going to die."

He falls onto his bed, looking up at the hole in the ceiling. I pull back so the flickering lantern light does not glint off my face.

"We're all going to die, Tony, though at your age it's still a theoretical concept."

"Mitch's dad forbids him to see me—ever again. He caught us under the stairs, just kissing, for Pete's sake."

He pounds the bed with his fists. Then he whimpers.

"Be cool, Tony. The first broken heart seems like it will never heal. But it does."

"I don't want to hear this," he says defiantly, getting to his feet and standing right beneath the hole.

"You want comfortable lies?"

"No, but why is the truth always so depressing?"

"Not always," I tell him, "just mostly. You will have other loves and other heartaches. But you're a brave kid. I know you're tough. You'll survive."

"I don't want to survive. I want to die."

"Too easy, Tony. Besides, there'll be times so stellar that no shadow can dim them, even in memory."

He rips the leather bracelet from his wrist and flings it into a corner.

"There will never be anyone else," he squalls.

I want to tell him the two shortest spans of time are *always* and *never*.

"But there will be others, my boy. Would you like to know their names?"

I envision several faces and know who they are, but whether they are in my past or Tony's future, I can't say.

Tony goes to his chest of drawers and takes out his flashlight. He aims it up at the hole.

"I bet I know who you are. You're like the ghost from Dickens' story—the ghost of the future, my future. Do you remember me, Mr. Six?"

"You do remind me of someone, Tony."

"Will you stay with me, Mr. Six? I mean be nearby, wherever I go? I have no one else to talk to except my Mom. Sometimes we read to each other. But I can't talk to my Dad. I feel so lonely sometimes. And I'm afraid."

"It's a brave man who admits his fear and carries on."

"Well, if you're my personal ghost, Mr. Six, then I should be able to take you along no matter where I move, right? Even if I wind up living in a basement flat, you'd still be my ghost in the attic."

"I'll do my best, my boy," I assure him, "but I'm not sure how it works. Rules are meant to be broken, though, right?"

He turns down the lantern and strips to his boxers. He lies on his back on the scratchy blanket. The recollection gives me a shiver.

"OK, Tony," I tell him. "I promise I'll be there, even if you can only hear me in your head."

"Good night, Mr. Six."

Whether I'm the ghost of the boy's future or he the ghost of my past, it's impossible to say.

I close the book I was reading and dim the old railroad lantern hanging from a bent nail in the rafter beside my bed. Lightning flashes in the distance, but I sleep through the storm.

Epilogue

"There are only two ways to live your life. One is as though nothing is a miracle. The other is as though everything is a miracle."
— Albert Einstein

The poem quoted herein is "Nightmare" by the Italian poet Bapellio who spent the summer of 1816 in the company of Lord Byron, Polidori, and the Shelleys on Lake Geneva, Switzerland, where Mary Shelley wrote "Frankenstein."

WEIRD SANTA

My parents were an odd pair. My mother was a former Catholic nun, though not yet former at the time of my conception. My father owned a pizza joint near Columbia University at the time my mother worked on finishing her doctorate in astrophysics, compliments of the Benedictines. They fell deeply in love despite struggling against it. They enjoyed their honeymoon here in dusty old Red Willow, New Mexico, and never went back to New York City.

What they had in common eluded everyone save an oddball friend they shared. His name was Nicolás, pronounced in the Spanish way. I have not witnessed a happier union than my parents' in my three decades on the planet. Their love was an elemental force and its warming rays enfolded me as well.

I'm proud to have my mother's intelligence and my father's calm control. My father, even when it was clear he was right, would say, "Oh, they'll discover their mistake." He was far from weak, but his patience exasperated my mother and me. My mother on the other hand, at the slightest slight, fired off incomprehensible volleys at full volume until she sounded as though she'd gone mad. My position between them meant that I tolerated an awful lot of crap, but when my lid blew, the explosion could be heard for miles.

My appearance melded my mother's flaxen-haired Nordic beauty and my father's curly-haired Mediterranean swarthiness. On most days I felt attractive, but on others I considered myself a girl designed by committee.

On my fourteenth birthday, my mother and father, Hildegarde and Oscar, told me what a "stellar young woman" I was "evolving" into. Those were their words.

"You seem as capable of taking care of yourself as I was at that age," my mother told me, failing to mention at my age she resided in the cushy digs of the Benedictine Order House in Binghamton, New York. "The time has come for your father and I to fulfill our own destinies. I'm afraid we must leave you."

"Leave? For how long?" I asked.

My father turned and looked at her.

"Probably forever, my dear, sweet child. We're going up The Mountain."

"What're you saying?" I realized I sounded whiny.

"We will be following our shaman to the top of The Mountain to learn how to bring the world into existence each morning. It takes many years of study. We must stay on when the old holy man dies."

I knew by my father's tone that their minds were made up. I suppressed a grin. *C'mon. Really? A shaman?* I thought, and started to cry.

"You'll be very well provided for," my father said, unable to look me quite in the eye.

"Mom. Dad. Are you serious? I'm fourteen years old. Not yet. Please," I begged.

"Well, then, when, Hypatia?" my mother asked. "Many children lose their parents at a much younger age. We want you to have plenty of time to become who you are, dear, without our getting in your way."

"Gee, thanks. How 'bout three more years?" I asked, trying not to sound too pathetic.

They glanced at each other and then at me. They nodded.

"You have us for another three years, child," my father said, giving me a gentle hug and a kiss slightly salty with tears.

My mother hugged us both. Ever the practical one of the pair, she advised me, "And please don't waste us on silly teenage tantrums, dear. Grow out of them before we go away. You can have them later in life if you like. Many of our friends do. Red Willow's just the place."

It was some of the best advice I ever received. They were the three happiest years of my life, too—at least so far. And, contrary to what I expected, I miss my parents more as time goes by, not less.

⊷◉⊶

On my seventeenth birthday, at our little family party before my friends arrived, my father handed me a thick investment portfolio carefully wrapped in sappy birthday paper.

"You will never have to worry, dear child."

"I don't anyway, Daddy. It doesn't change anything; a total waste of time."

"God bless you, Hypatia, wise beyond your years," my mother remarked.

My mother handed me her own small package. It contained the deed to their house and the keys to her eighteen-inch Newtonian telescope, to the motorized drives that moved the beast. She lost her composure and ran to my father, burying her face in his shoulder and sobbing.

I nearly broke down myself when I was saved by the doorbell. It was my friend Ginnie from school. She held a shiny foil package tied with sparkling red ribbon—entirely her style. My parents introduced themselves and then disappeared into the kitchen.

When the bell rang again, it was their strange friend, the skinny old guy the rest of town called "Weird Santa." Now I knew who their "shaman" was. I pointed Nicolás—if that was his name—towards the kitchen. I heard them exchange blessings, and then the back door closed. I told my friend Ginnie my parents were running away from home.

"Oh, my God," she screeched. "What're you going to do?"

"Uh, let me see. My parents will be out of the house, not coming back. I have the keys to the liquor cabinet. My friends are coming over. What d'you think I'm going to do?"

"Aren't you sorry?" Ginnie asked.

"Of course I am," I told her. "But that won't bring them back. I'm trying to make the most of my changed life. What d'you expect? I'm a teenager."

The doorbell rang. It was Helen and Alice and Alice's ugly, big-eared boyfriend. Word must have spread. Someone invited a Turkish techno band called Brief Heavy Downpours who played loud enough to crack two windows. There was no one the neighbors could complain to any longer. I was now the majordoma. Too bad.

Somebody brought pizza, but it wasn't from my Dad's place. It was pretty bad. I had a long make-out with a boy I didn't like and sampled more flavors of alcohol than I knew existed, including one with a worm in the bottle which the boy I didn't like coaxed me into swallowing. It must have been the worm. I spent the night and next morning in the bathroom.

When I awoke at the crack of noon, I was alone in the big old hacienda. I thought of my parents and cried for three hours—on and off, but mostly on—until I was as dry as the desert wind blowing into Red Willow. I haven't touched alcohol since. Or worms.

I never laid eyes on my mother and father again.

I remained convinced the odd fellow who followed my parents from New York and hung around the house every year at Christmas was the same guy everyone in town called "Weird Santa." I know he had something to do with getting the behemoth Newtonian telescope from upstate New York out here to New Mexico from my mother's Order House.

Nearly all the citizens of Red Willow had an encounter with Weird Santa at least once in their lives. It was certain his mottled gray-and-white beard was genuine, yet no one in town sported such chin whiskers. Where did he hide out the rest of the time? Many of us had received one of his insanely appropriate Christmas gifts, meticulously wrapped geometric solids that bore no relation to the shape of the object inside. He knew each of us by name and remembered enough of our circumstances to qualify as more than a casual acquaintance. The *Red Willow Reporter* offered a one-thousand-dollar prize to the person who could unequivocally identify him. It has gone unclaimed for the past five years.

Last December, a dozen years after my parents went away, I stayed with my friend Ginnie in Santa Fe the week before Christmas. She had a boutique of hand-made punk turquoise jewelry, all of it too big and painfully ugly. It was wildly popular, and she was considering opening a second shop in Red Willow. Weird Santa accosted me in the parking lot and added another bundle to my overladen arms.

"Your mother and father are very well, Hypatia. They are quite adept at calling up the moon and it is only a matter of time before they can call up the sun by themselves. Stay warm, child."

Before I could peek around the packages he was gone, up the street handing out a box in silver foil to another bewildered shopper. I dropped his present fumbling with my car keys. It did not appear to be broken: nothing tinkled or rattled. I set my purchases in the back of the car and unwrapped it. One box nested inside another like Russian dolls. The gift was a log, not even a whole log, but a split log. *Just what I need*, I thought, and put it back among the other packages.

It began to snow around Española and did not let up for the rest of the drive home. The temperature had plummeted, too. I was eager to get warm and snug.

A yellow sticker hung from the front doorknob. It did not look like good news. I fetched the presents and the half-log from Weird Santa and rushed inside.

The house was freezing, probably just a degree or two above the pipes bursting. The notice on the door had been a disconnect order from the gas company. Just great. And no one available for the next three days to reconnect my service—and my heat.

It was exactly like my latest ex, Elliot, to maintain his nano music service but forget to pay the gas bill. He'd left two weeks before, saving me the trouble of kicking his ass out at Christmas. His crap was already rotting in the Eco-Happy Landfill. I felt much more agreeable since he left, the best Christmas present he could have given me. But it was good-bye to boyfriend number five, the fifth in five years, each one's name beginning with the letter "E," the fifth letter. I wondered, *Was there some kind of message here or was every datable man in Red Willow a loser with the intellectual life of a mushroom?*

I put the log from Weird Santa in the fireplace in the kiva and lit it with the paper and cardboard from its wrappings. It caught quickly and put out a good deal of heat for its size. I stretched out my fingers. I would be warm for ten minutes. What then? And I'd have to drain the water system before the pipes froze. Merry Fucking Christmas.

That dear little yule log continued to pump out heat and a cheering glow for three more hours. I gave up before the fire did and went to bed. Even my bedroom, furthest from the kiva, was toasty. I was beyond figuring it out just then. Weird Santa's gift was insanely appropriate. He'd known exactly what I needed. Merry Christmas.

<hr/>

It is Christmas Eve again, a year later, my second holiday season without a boyfriend. If Weird Santa wants to bring me something I can really use, it'd be a man. I'm not ready to settle yet for just any man, though maybe I might in another week.

I regret there is still no boyfriend Number Six, but maybe that's for the best. I had many wonderful Christmases with my parents. It's the one time of year I associate particularly with them and their weird friend. I miss them, and I don't need another know-it-all boyfriend spoiling Christmas for me and getting me upset.

The log from Weird Santa is still burning twelve months later. It must be impregnated with some nasty petrochemicals, but it beats hauling firewood, cleaning out ashes, and choking on smoke. I don't know what's going on, but I'm sure it's not magical. My parents, I'm afraid, believed in such nonsense, and unusual abilities some called "paranormal" were ascribed to them. I lived with them for seventeen years and never witnessed anything that wasn't normal parental weirdness. Well, except maybe once.

I wanted to know if my parents were still doing it, you know, making love. I waited until I heard their bedroom door close, and sneaked around to the *portalo* at the back of the house and peeked through the window. They had candles burning everywhere. It was miraculous they didn't burn the house down. My parents floated several feet above their bed, nearly reaching the *vigas* on the ceiling, the sheets still wrapped around their legs and dangling down.

I ran from the sight. It scared me. But I never thought it was anything other than a mechanical contraption, probably of my mother's devising, to enhance their love-making. I supposed when you're in your forties you needed all the help you can get. My parents raised me to be a true skeptic. There's nothing and no one I believe without unequivocal proof, even my dear mother and father. I never violated their privacy again no matter how bad curiosity had bit me.

———————◦———————

I glance up at the creche that was my mother's on the narrow ledge above the hive-shaped hearth. It is the only item I possess to mark Christmas. The scene depicts an ordinary family fallen on hard times, to me, but they are held together by their love and they will make it.

I laugh remembering my first serious boyfriend Edward's coming over here at Christmas six years ago. He told me the creche was idolatry and my little live-potted Xmas tree was a pagan symbol used to invoke the devil. What a spoilsport. How to put a damp blanket on Christmas cheer.

"Then how about gingerbread men?" I asked him. "Does it promote cannibalism, you know, like the Last Supper?"

"Don't be ridiculous, Hypatia. You need to call on Jesus and beg His forgiveness."

"The hell with Jesus and the ass he rode in on," I told him.

Edward sputtered as though all the circuits in his brain

were misfiring. He never got the words out. I grabbed his coat from a peg by the front door and threw it down the walkway after him. It landed in a puddle of slush: not my intention, but I wasn't sorry, either. What a drip.

I get up to make a cup of ginger tea with honey. It is only four o'clock and the sun is already setting. I remember what one of the old horsemen from the Pueblo said about the white man and Daylight Savings Time. He remarked it was like cutting one end off a blanket and sewing onto the opposite end to make it longer.

I pull my favorite chair in the kiva nearer the fire. Recalling boyfriends seems to be the theme of the evening. I take a sip of tea and give the perpetual log a little poke simply out of habit. It perks up a bit and I nestle into the chair.

Feeling I had learned my lesson dating a Christian, I found it easy to fall for Ephraim, a Jew from Santa Fe whose parents wrote a three-volume set on the diaspora in New Mexico. At least he could quote a few things not in the Talmud. He was a sweet man who didn't push his religion. I found other things to do on his Sabbath. But his dietary proscriptions drove me crazy.

Like a devoted girlfriend, I learned to cook according to his requirements, not that it occurred to me he might accommodate himself to a couple of my customs. That year I went all-out making and baking the Christmas foods I remembered as a girl, but done according to his religion—mostly. I liked him a lot, even if actual love was still on the back burner.

"What are these tiny red specks in the scalloped potatoes, Hypatia?" he asked.

"Small bits of bacon," I told him.

"Bacon!" he screamed.

"Let loose a little, Ephraim. It's Christmas. Besides, I'm pretty sure it's kosher bacon."

"Kosher bacon? Are you trying to send me to Gehinnom?"

I stood up and slammed down the casserole baking dish so hard it cracked in half. I nudged Ephraim up out of his chair and escorted him by the elbow to the front door.

"No, just trying to get you out my house and out of my life. Your going to purgatory is up to Jehovah and, from what I read, he doesn't like anybody. He's a mean old white man with hemorrhoids and an electric finger."

I flung his jacket after him, knocking his yarmulke, his beanie, into a half-melted puddle. Well, maybe I'd been aiming that time.

In the last of the day's light I see it is snowing lightly: big, fluffy flakes. It is supposed to develop into a fairly strong storm with a foot of snow possible by morning. I am glad I have nowhere to go tonight, though I wouldn't mind if someone visited me.

With boyfriend Number Three, I eschewed Christians and Jews, and sidestepped Muslims and Mormons, and went straight for a born-again atheist. I consulted an analyst for my depression and sorry love-life, but it developed rather quickly into something more. I thought it might be unethical, but the doctor assured me no one would know. I wasn't quite sure what that had to do with my therapy.

Dr. Egad De Bockel came to Red Willow a decade before from Holland and set up his practice to serve well-heeled clients— as in high-heels. They came here from the big cities in Colorado, Texas, and California. He assured me I was living in a "hat-sized fable" and that I could have any man I put my mind to wanting, even him.

Egad was a far better lover than either Edward or Ephraim, and he treated me as though I were special to him in ways beyond mere doctor-patient. I was naive back then and fell in love with his handsome goatee which he employed to tickle me into howling ecstasy.

Dr. De Bockel did not believe in God, but he had his own religion of psychiatry in which everything I did meant something else. I started saying the opposite of what I intended in hopes he might mistakenly take it the right way. I became so tangled in knots and subterfuges that I thought of seeing another analyst to get myself sorted out, but it felt like cheating.

The break-up with Egad happened once more on Christmas Eve. He questioned why I had a little tree with lights in the kiva.

"That tree is a symbol of gross capitalistic commercialism. It doesn't belong in the home of any sane person who doesn't believe in fairy stories," he chortled.

"Listen, you affected windbag," I replied, "that gross commercialism pays your way. If not for capitalism, there'd be no one with money to fritter away on getting analyzed, that's for sure. They'd have to consult a genuine witch doctor who'd at least shrink their heads for real."

Dr. De Bockel huffed and puffed and swelled himself up like an indignant blowfish. He stormed out the front door. Halfway down the walk, he turned for his tweedy little hat. I tossed it to him like a frisbee. The hat circled around his head and plopped in a patch of mud. I hadn't meant it, but that did nothing to keep me from laughing hysterically.

———◦———

It appears I will have to spend this Christmas alone. I decide to soothe myself with a hot bubble bath and a second cup of ginger tea. The instant I turn off the tap, ready to climb in, I hear a crash from the kiva that sounds like the perpetual log tumbling out of the fireplace. I grab my bathrobe from the hook and go to investigate.

Soot fans out from the hearth. I discover a plate of sugar cookies and glass of milk sitting on the coffee table. It has to be Weird Santa. He's got it ass-backwards.

Besides the milk and cookies, he's left a package in luminescent paper beside the hearth. The fire feels good. I hold the present against my breasts and turn around to warm my backside. I pull at the illuminated ribbon. The present puffs up several times in size but remains flat. It feels like heavy fabric or leather.

What tumbles from the neon paper is what appears to be

a vinyl pool inflatable in the shape of a man. I stretch it to its full length: about six feet, anatomically correct. It makes me laugh. The laughter feels good on Christmas Eve. I guess I got my wish after all.

"Merry Christmas, Weird Santa," I holler up the flue, knowing he went to a bit of trouble to make it look like that's how he'd come and gone.

The inflatable is a sickly pinkish color, not quite opaque, and he's a ginger. The valve is where you might expect. Naughty old Santa. The foreskin is the valve cap. I laugh so hard I cannot get any air into my new blow-up beau.

I revisit my memory of Number Four, the tortured Goth poet too frail to consider manual labor, which he saw as demeaning. He affected to be the Edgar Allen Ginsberg of Goth poetry. His poems, all the rage among the trust-fund hippies of Red Willow, were depressing. He was depressing.

We spent Christmas Eve together two years ago, the year before Elliot. I came home late after staying to help my friend Ginnie in her punk jewelry boutique. Edgar sat in the kiva stark naked, all but tapping his foot with impatience.

"Where were you?" he asked, glowering.

"Earning our daily bread, dearest. Ginnie stayed open late. We had customers."

Edgar stood up, growing erect, and motioned me to my knees. I was in no mood. I hoped his ass was getting cold. I put my lips around the tip of his penis.

"You are an imbecile, Hypatia. You are so literal. Blow job is just an expression, an idiom. What do you think will be accomplished by blowing?"

"That I'd get out of having to give you a blow job, you jerk. Out. Right now."

I pushed him by degrees toward the front door and opened it for him.

"Hypatia, are you crazy? It's snowing."

I gave him a playful push and he sprawled in an icy puddle. Before he could scramble back up the walkway, I flung his car keys at him and wished him a Happy Holiday. Pulling the blinds helped conserve heat. I donated his clothes to the homeless shelter.

———————◦◦———————

I light the old railroad lantern that had been my father's. It casts a cheering glow. Weird Santa's yule log flares a little. I feel sleepy, and light-headed from blowing up the manikin. It is nearly fully inflated. I lie down on my back and put my head against his belly, feeling comfy and warm. I fall asleep, wishing I had wished to see my parents again instead.

———————◦◦———————

I awake startled and gasping for air. The Inflatable Man has moved, or at least it seemed like it in my half-wakeful state. I must have poked a hole in him. I hear a leak, like a sigh. I turn around. His chest heaves slowly and rhythmically. This is one realistic toy. I wonder where Weird Santa got it. Ginnie would get a hoot out of having one.

The blow-up dummy's eyes open and it sits up. I jump up and grab the poker, brandishing it like Hypatia the Amazon. He does not seem the least bit threatened.

"All right, buster, get up. Better move slowly or I'll bash your head in."

"Why do wish to hurt me, Hypatia? I am your Christmas present. Don't you want to play with me before you break me?"

It turns its head and looks at me. I lean forward and rest my hand on its shoulder. It is warm and firm, not like a hollow man, a balloon man. It must be a robotic toy. *But how did it come all flat and folded up like that?* I wonder.

"You breathed life into me," it says in a beautiful baritone. "Now I am yours."

Yeah, in my dreams, I think.

"But you are awake," it says.

Oh, so, a toy that reads minds, I beam at it.

"I am not a toy. I am a man."

His penis swells and inches upward.

"Did Weird Santa send you?"

"Santa Nicolás brought me, yes, but you breathed life into me. I am yours."

What is going on, I ask myself.

"It is Christmas. I am your present. Let's be friends."

He sounds like a Forrest Gump simpleton.

"I find it hard to believe in Christmas. It's mostly for children," I tell him.

"Then be a child, Hypatia."

"Please don't tell me what to do, uh… uh… What's your name?"

"I don't have one until you give me a name."

I think for a minute. It will most definitely not begin with the letter "E."

"How about 'Number Six,'" I suggest. "*Six* for short."

"I am Six," he says, beaming with pride.

His voice reminds me of a cello: resonant, deep, and sad. His beautiful, rugged body distracts me so that I can no longer concentrate on keeping straight what's real and what isn't. I tell him to sit by the fire while I look for something of Elliot's to hang on Six's well-built frame.

I open the bottom drawers of the chest where Elliot kept some of his old clothes, hoping I might have overlooked something. He was about the same size. There's a worn pair of Levi's and a threadbare gray gym sweatshirt. I just hope nothing rubs off. I like Six just as he is.

Six gets into the jeans and sweatshirt, and I swear he is almost as sexy with his clothes on. We lie opposite each other on the sofa and wiggle our bare feet beneath the cushions. Six pulls a slightly tattered blanket over us. It has one end cut off and sewn coarsely to the other.

"Where did this come from, Six?"

"I guess it must be my baby blanket," he says, breaking into a grin.

"There's something you're not telling me."

"I am the gift, you are the recipient, Santa Nicolás is the messenger, and your parents are the givers."

"You saw them?"

"Not actually, but they send you their love. They have sent me to you as an expression of their love. I am your present. I am yours now, all yours."

I am too tired to argue or probe further. Moving to lie next to him, I snuggle against his chest. Six wraps his arms around me. Knowing he came from my parents, I feel comfortable and safe. I fall asleep listening to his heartbeat.

------------------◦◦------------------

I awake alone, tangled in the tattered blanket. The sofa is not the best place for a long lie-down. I knew it had to be a dream, and feel sorry that someone like Six is not real. I smell bacon frying and sit bolt upright on the lumpy sofa. There is clattering in the kitchen.

Six is at the stove frying bacon and making a large omelet with jalapeños and cheese. Bread pops up from the toaster, and he reaches for butter and cherry jam. He senses my standing there and turns around, switching on his smile.

"Merry Christmas, Hypatia. Are you hungry?"

"I'm famished."

"Go sit down. I'll bring it to the table."

He pours a mug of coffee and, adding a splash of cream, hands it to me. Somehow he knows how I like my coffee. He brings a tray with two plates of toast, omelet, and three strips of bacon each. He seems amused by my voracious appetite, watching me intently as I devour each mouthful. We discuss plans for a Christmas supper and manage to agree on everything. I'm sure the real Six will turn up sooner or later, the one with the horns.

After breakfast, he hurries off with the dishes. He begins washing them and I point out to him there is a dishwasher.

"I do not know how to operate one," he tells me. "Do you need a license?"

"My ex seemed to think so, but, no, you don't need a license as long as it stays in the house."

He doesn't realize I'm joking. I find that endearing somehow. I head off to the bathroom. The bubble bath from the night before has gone flat. I decide to have a long shower instead, for as long as the meager hot water holds out.

I shut my eyes and let the soothing water stream over my face. Ahh. When I open them again, Six is peeking around the shower curtain, smiling at me.

"Why don't you hop in?" I tell him. "No. Take your clothes off first."

"Right," he says.

Six's skin is less puckered. He has filled out nicely and his flesh tone looks more natural. It is browner. His hair, too, is now more auburn. He is quite a specimen of manhood.

Six steps into the shower and giggles like a boy. He wiggles around and tries to get behind me.

"It tickles," he howls.

I wouldn't be surprised if it were his first shower. The water seems to bring out his "new" smell, like something starched or sized when it gets wet. I show him how to adjust the stream by turning the shower head. I have never known a man willing, even eager, to learn something from a woman. It's a first. He thanks me. Am I dreaming now? I don't know whether to stick myself or him with a pin. Will I wake up? Will he deflate?

Six takes the washcloth and soap from me and begins washing my breasts. He lets the washcloth drop and continues with just his hands and the bar of soap. It is exhilarating, then exciting. He washes me everywhere, slowly, caressingly. He tilts my head back and shampoos my hair, running his fingers through it, pulling me back beneath the water to rinse me off.

"Your turn," I say.

As soon as I touch him with the soapy rag, he laughs. He jumps around so much I could hold the washcloth still and let him do the work. I think the soap has gotten rid of that "new man" smell. When I cup his penis in my soapy hands, his little friend wakes from his slumber.

Six lifts me by my waist and I put my arms around his neck and wrap my legs around his hips. Despite the slightly awkward position, he enters me with ease. His movements are masterful: no need for instruction here. He knows precisely what I want. He has the loping grace and rhythm of a cat, of a mountain lion.

At the moment of our shared climax, the shower grows noticeably warmer, steamy hot. I experience an orgasm throughout my body, everywhere Six has touched me, everywhere the water flows, from my ears to my toes. I look deep into his eyes.

"It is hard to breathe," he says.

"Yes, that happens," I tell him. "Next time, we'll go a little slower."

After our shower, Six enfolds me in a warm towel and rubs me dry. I scurry off to the bedroom. The house feels chilly after the hot shower. *Where'd he get a warm towel?* I wonder. The man is full of mysteries.

I get dressed in a green skirt and red sweater, going intentionally sappy for Christmas. I find a pair of stretched-out old wool hiking socks for Six. He's in the kitchen preparing the supper we'd discussed, dressed again in the old jeans and sweatshirt. I hand him the oversized socks. He puts them on, then goes back to stirring something in a saucepan.

All the supper choices are mine except one. Six wanted to make gingerbread cookies. He's a gentle and agreeable man. I hope I'm not railroading him.

"Tomorrow we have to get you boots and a jacket," I tell him. "And gloves."

"That would be nice," he says.

"Sure it would when I'm the one paying," I grouse.

"I came here with nothing. I came here empty, Hypatia. These are not even my clothes. You gave me everything and you filled me up. I have only myself to give you."

I put my arms around him and cry into his shoulder.

"I did not mean to be so mean, Six. I'm sorry, especially on Christmas."

He wipes my tears with his thumbs.

"It is time for the gingerbread men to be born," he says.

He opens the oven and grabs the cookie sheet with his bare hand. I scream, but he does not seem hurt and does not react to my loud cry. Instead, he smiles. Maybe he thinks it was a squeal of delight. He certainly has a high tolerance for heat.

The aroma of gingerbread made with real ginger returns me to girlhood. Six scoops white frosting into a pastry bag, twists it closed, and hands it to me. I begin decorating the gingerbread men. I give them tiny male appendages. Six laughs. I have not had this much fun at Christmas since my parents went away.

When I've put icing on roughly half the cookies, Six takes the pastry bag from me and decorates the remaining asexual ones. These he gives sugary breasts and little vaginal "V"s.

"If I put the cookie sheets back in the oven, maybe we'll get a bunch of gingerbread kids," he suggests.

It is his first intentional joke. Six hands me a steaming mug of ginger tea—prepared when I wasn't paying attention—and waves me toward the kiva.

A second squall of snow has begun, already a few inches, yet the flagstone walkway is perfectly clear. I ask Six when he shoveled.

"After our shower and before making supper," he tells me.

"But the walkway is still dry."

"It must still be warm."

"Warm?" I ask him.

"Here, taste this," he remarks, putting a spoon to my lips.

I don't know if he's trying to distract me or really wants to know what I think of his sauce for the scalloped potatoes. In either case it worked. It's delicious. I return to my mug of tea. I feel like a child again: warm and cozy and cared for. It is my fervent wish not to have to send Six down the walkway on Christmas—or any other day.

———◦◦◦———

I awaken from my doze. Six stands at the hearth. He hears me and turns around. The perpetual yule log flares up even though he has no tools in his hands and the screen is closed. The wind moans. I become engulfed in scrumptious aromas, each of them distinct, and breathe them in.

"Come, Hypatia. Our meal is ready," he says, offering me a

hand to get up from the sofa.

I open the oven and peek at the beautifully crisped roast duckling. The orange and honey sauce bubbles on a back burner. The casserole dish of scalloped potatoes garnished with bits of bacon and parsley sits on the tile counter. A loaf of bread, bursting from its pan, sits on the cutting board.

"Have a seat," Six tells me. "Let me serve you."

He brings in bowls and platters of food, including a perfectly carved duck. He sits down across from me in the dining area, his chest puffed out with pride.

"It is beautiful, Six," I tell him. "Oh, please don't forget the candles."

As I scoot my chair closer, I see a flash at the corner of my eye. Six is withdrawing his finger from the now-burning candle.

"You lit that with your finger, didn't you," I tell him more than ask him.

"Yes," he admits.

"And the yule log and the hot shower and the walkway and the warm towel?"

"Yes, yes, yes, yes."

"How do you do it?"

"I don't know," he replies. "But I can't keep supper warm forever. You must say a thanksgiving. It is customary."

"Why me?"

"We are beneath your roof."

I am speechless, a condition my father believed impossible. Many impossible things happen at Christmas, I guess, and if they happen then they must be possible.

"I thank my parents, Oscar and Hildegarde, for building this roof over our heads, for providing this wonderful meal with the proceeds from stock sales, but most of all for the man they sent me who made every tidbit and morsel with love. And Merry Christmas to Weird Santa Nicolás, too, whoever he is."

Six touches my lips with his finger.

"Thank you," he says, and scoops a heap of steaming potatoes onto my plate.

Throughout the meal I glance past Six at the gingerbread

people on their cookie sheets on the tile counter behind him, basking like naked sunbathers. I couldn't possibly bite off an arm or a leg or a head. I plot to save them.

"Why don't we get a little Christmas tree tomorrow?" I suggest. "They'll probably be free, since it will be the day after. We'll cut our own."

"That would be fun," Six replies, licking orange sauce from his fingers.

"I'll get red and green ribbon and we'll hang the gingerbread cookies on the tree," I add.

"OK," he agrees. "Then we can admire them every evening with a glass of milk after supper."

I laugh. If Six learns any faster, I may find it hard to keep up with him.

A CHANGE OF HEART

I've no idea where I am going or where I've been. It doesn't matter. I keep going toward the lights. I walk at the edge of the road in dusty Levi's, jean jacket, and cowboy boots that look as though they'd traversed the entire Southwest diagonally. I've got a drum-banging headache.

I cross the highway to the Sagebrush Diner, no traffic in either direction as far as the eye can see. I am famished. The two cars and three pickup trucks in the gravel lot all bear New Mexico license tags. The newest is a cream-colored Hudson from about 1947. I'm not sure how I know this. It's a classy set of wheels. It drives away before I get to the diner.

The five men at the counter are dressed similarly in dusty boots and blue jeans. I leave an empty seat beside the last man and sit down on the next red leatherette stool.

"What'll it be, Six?" the ginger-haired waitress asks. She looks over her glasses at me.

I wonder for a minute how she knows me. Is it because I am the sixth man at the counter? In the quilted stainless steel wall behind her, with the pass-through to the kitchen, I see my distorted reflection. On my faded blue T-shirt is a backward white number six.

"The usual, Fanny," I say, taking a chance I know her, too. Her name is embroidered on her white blouse.

"You got 'er."

Each of the five men at the counter nods at me in the shiny

diamond-pattern wall.

"Mornin', Six," recites the male chorus.

I'm pleased to note I am not disliked in these parts. Fanny whisks past, leaving a welcome cup of black coffee. She turns the handle towards my left hand. I pick it up and inhale the steam before swallowing. It clears my head. I feel as though I've awakened after sleeping for twenty years, except that I've awakened in the past, not the future.

I think of eggs and thick bacon and a stack of flapjacks drowning in peach syrup. Fanny sets the heavy china plate in front of me—exactly as I'd craved—and refills my coffee. I'm beginning to like it here. I remove my cowboy hat and set it on the empty stool.

"Where's Antonio today?" one of the men asks, leaning forward across the counter and cocking his head toward the empty seat beside me.

"And where's your truck? You need a jump or somethin'?" asks the second man at the counter.

Fanny stops in her constant back-and-forth and puts her hands on her ample hips.

"Let him eat his breakfast, y'all," she tells them.

I'm off the hook; I don't know the answers to their questions. She turns to the pass-through and loads her arms up with plates of food for one of the booths by the window. From the conversation up and down the counter I learn that the Korean War is about to commence. It is June of 1950. I shiver.

Fanny stops on her way back behind the counter and stands beside me with the speckled blue enamel coffee pot.

"Six. What'd you do to the back of your head? There's dried blood all over your collar. And your hat," she adds, picking it up and turning it over.

The five men at the counter get up and stand around me in an arc buzzing like drones, talking all at once.

"Maybe you better see Doc Morgan."

"That's quite a goose-egg."

"Phineas'll drive you home, Six."

"There's nothing getting between me and these flapjacks

until they're all safely packed away," I tell them, brushing aside the many hands eager to help.

They sit back down while I finish my breakfast. The conversation, now more hushed, returns to the Communists. When I swallow the last of my coffee, I am all but lifted out of my seat by a man at either elbow. They escort me to the door. I reach for my wallet, but it is not in my hip pocket. Where else would it be?

"You settle up later," Fanny tells me. "And though I know it don't matter much to bachelors, you soak your shirt and jacket in cold water and crush in a couple aspirins."

"Yes, Ma'am," I tell her.

The others laugh, holding me firmly as we descend the five steps from the Sagebrush Diner to the dusty lot. They get me into the cab of a dark blue Ford pickup and sandwich me between the driver and the second fellow, who keeps his arm around my shoulder so I don't tip over.

The dirt road to wherever it is I live is potholed and deeply rutted. Steering seems pointless. My head bounces and bobs, and my headache gets louder. A plume of dust billows behind us. There is still snow on the mountain to the east, but I don't remember its name.

We come to a stop beside a small, two-storey adobe house with deep, tin-roofed portalos in front and back. There is a corral, but I see no horses. Chickens run in and out of the leaning, unpainted barn. I'd be surprised if the barn roof didn't leak, too. This is where I live?

When the two men—Phineas and Mitch, as I learn—get me down out of the pickup and on my feet, I realize I am not going to make it. The house and the corral and the enormous cottonwood tree overhead swirl as though they're about to spin down a drain. I see the front door swing open, but that is the last I recall.

———◦———

I awake on my back with a cool rag over my eyes and forehead. I can tell my boots and jean jacket have been removed. I attempt to sit up. My head throbs.

"Easy, buddy," a male voice intones. "Go slow."

The damp cloth falls from my face. The man is a handsome mestizo with the best features of both worlds. He has sun-browned skin and longish hair that is so black it looks almost blue. He extends his forearm to help me sit up.

"The waitress at the diner says to soak my jacket in cold water," I tell him.

"It's already hanging outside. I thought we'd lost you when you didn't come home last night, Six. Doc Morgan's been here. He said you've got to rest."

I feel a bandage taped to the back of my head and wonder how I will pay for a doctor's visit. I ask the man if he is my nurse or something.

"Among other things," he says, smiling. "Let's get you under the covers."

The man lifts up my T-shirt and carefully slips it past the wound at the back of my head. I unbutton my Levi's and he pulls them off me. Then he takes my socks. When he reaches for the waistband of my longjohns, I stop his hands. I can feel they are used to work.

"I'll keep 'em on," I tell him.

The man looks at me and shrugs. He swings my legs off the side of the bed, tugs back the covers, and pivots me back around. Then he pulls the sheet and quilt up to my neck. He leans forward and gets right up to my face like he's going to kiss me. I turn my head away. The man pulls back and stands up.

"I'm going to be downstairs so you get some rest, Six. Don't try coming down on your own. Call me—for anything. And use the chamber pot if you've gotta go. Good night, buddy."

The neighbor, or whoever he is, turns off the electric lamp on the bed table and lights an old railroad lantern with a match. The sulphur stings my nose. He sets the lantern atop the small dresser in the corner. It casts just the right light, enough to see where I'm going in a strange house, but not so bright it keeps me awake. When he reaches the doorway, I ask him if he knows who Antonio is. The question stops him in his tracks.

"Boy, you really clunked your noggin a good one, Six. I'm

Antonio. The Doc said it'll all come back to you. Now get to sleep."

He pulls the door partway closed and shoots me a wink over his shoulder. I close my eyes. His face is vaguely familiar, but I cannot recall a thing about him. I trust it will sort itself out in the morning.

I am awakened when Antonio jostles me. He is dressed in fresh jeans and a denim workshirt. I smell food. There is a speckled enamel plate on the bed table. It is steaming.

"I've got to get to work, Six. With both of us off yesterday, Nicolás will be frantic. Make sure you eat that. I'll be home at lunch."

"We work together?" I ask.

"Among other things," Antonio replies.

He seems to like that answer. He again leans over me, as though to kiss me good-bye. I quickly put the cup of coffee to my mouth. He stops, looking a little bewildered, and heads out the door. I hear a truck drive into the yard and the door downstairs closes. I sit up straighter in bed and set the plate in my lap. The tortillas are filled with scrambled eggs and beans, and flooded with cheese and green chilies. My appetite has not quite returned, but I do my best.

I eat distractedly. I'm not sure what's going on and why I remember so little. The plate is soon empty though I recall only the taste of the first bite. Once again sleepy, I lay back on the pillows. The more I try to think, the more my head hurts. I give up and surrender to sleep.

I awaken when Antonio sits down at the edge of the bed. He touches my hand. The light seems so bright, even with the curtains closed.

"You were sleeping so sound I didn't want to wake you for lunch. It's almost supper time."

"That explains why I'm so hungry," I say, and pull my hand away.

"I'm gonna get back to supper. Maybe you can take a bath. I've got water on the stove."

Antonio gives me an arm to hang onto and helps me up. He descends the stairs in front of me, ready to catch me in case I fall.

The kitchen and the rest of the first floor are one room. The old claw-foot tub is behind a faded curtain of palm fronds and tropical plants separating it from the kitchen proper. I see no indoor plumbing except for the pump at the kitchen sink. The tub drains through a rubber hose out to the garden.

He pours another bucket of hot water from the stove and tests the bath with his hand, declaring it warm enough. I step behind the curtain, recognizing myself in the shaving mirror on a nail in the wall. I'm nearly Antonio's opposite: fair-skinned and blond, but also sun-tanned.

"You can toss me your longjohns. I'll be doing laundry on Sunday."

"What don't you do around here?" I ask, but Antonio is back at the stove.

The water is hot. I descend into it slowly. I soap up the brush and washcloth, and enjoy feeling clean again. I forget about my wound and wince when I pour soapy water over my head with a chipped enamel mug. The bandage floats in the scummy water.

"How we doin'?" Antonio asks, pulling back the curtain.

I don't want to admit it, but I tell him I think I need help climbing out of the tub. I've got the same equipment Antonio does, so I swallow my embarrassment. I feel helpless.

He dries my back with the rough towel and hands it to me to finish the job. He puts clean clothes on the wooden stool beside the tub. He's brought me moccasins instead of my boots.

When I am dressed, I come to the table, just in time for him to set a huge plate of pinto beans and tomato salad and a pair of chicken enchiladas before me. I am ready to dive in, but Antonio closes his eyes and says grace. I bow my head, staring at the steaming food.

"They found the truck," Antonio tells me. "Over near Dry Gulch. Nothing wrong with it, Mitch says. Your wallet was in the glove box."

My mouth is too full to respond. I don't know what kind of truck I own, or even if I own it, and I've no idea whether there was money in my wallet. Antonio tries several times to find out whether I remember anything of what happened. I am far more interested in the dessert he's brought to the table: cherry jack *empanadas*, with green chilies in them. I know what most things are called, but I don't remember what they taste like, so I dive into the dessert.

"Nothing wrong with your appetite, either," he declares. "Doc said when you get your appetite back it's a good sign."

Antonio clears the table and puts another log in the stove for hot water for dishes. I offer to help, but he does not let me. He insists I go on up to bed. He takes my arm as we go up the stairs. I look at the small sofa—a settee, really—where he sleeps. The cushions look lumpy and the seat has caved in, the bottom almost touching the floor.

I let him help me undress down to my longjohns, but no man is pulling off my underwear as long as I can manage it myself. He dims the kerosene railroad lantern and smiles at me from the doorway before going downstairs. Each step has its own creak or squeak.

The clatter of dishes keeps me awake at first, but soon it becomes the rhythmic clacking of train tracks. I hear the mournful whistle in the distance—perhaps only the teakettle—and wonder when and where I will awaken, and how much I'll remember.

On Saturday Antonio and I drive to Mila-Grow Nursery & Greenhouse where we both work. Our truck is a 1941 Ford pickup which Antonio painted turquoise blue. It looks as if he used a coarse brush.

I'm introduced—or re-introduced—to the owner, Nicolás, who resembles a skinny, rumpled Santa Claus, his whiskers more gray than white. His accent is hard to understand. I nod my head even when I don't quite get it. He and Antonio exchange a couple of sentences in Spanish. Antonio intends to put in a full day, but he will drive me home at lunch. Then he walks out among the trees and shrubs and flowers.

"You getting better, Six, before you coming back to working," Nicolás tells me, putting his hand on my shoulder.

"How will I pay bills?" I ask him.

He laughs like there's something I'm not getting.

"But Antonio is working. Why do you worrying?"

"Sure," I say. "He's gonna pay all my bills for me, too."

"Él es tu amigo, no? And maybe I pay little something while you getting better."

"Thanks, Nicolás, but I pay my own way."

He shakes his head.

"No, you still not right, Six. You working when you getting better," he says, and walks out to the gardens.

I wander aimlessly up and down the rows of plants. I cannot name a single one. I run into Mitch from the diner and learn I am the resident expert on stonework: walls, ponds, and walkways. I also find out Antonio and I have shared the *casita* out on the mesa for the past three years, after serving our two years in the army, drafted right after high school. His *abuela* left the house to him. Nobody remembers a time Antonio and I were not best buddies.

Yeah, but does anyone think there's more to it than that? I want to ask. Mitch is not getting my drift. He reminds me Antonio and I get along really good, and pooling our wages makes us both richer. What more did I want?

Around noon the company pickup pulls in after the morning on the job, two men in front, two men and the shovels in back. They spill out and surround me, slapping me on the back. It feels good to have so many friends. They all talk at once.

"Easy, guys," Antonio warns them. "Six, I gotta get you home now. Let's go."

From the rear window I see the men waving as we pull out. They're all at least ten or fifteen years older than Antonio and me. The truck lurches and weaves, but I know it's the road and not Antonio's driving.

Back at the house, Antonio slices a chunk of salami from the larder and slaps it between two crusts of homemade bread.

"Make sure you eat something. You need help getting upstairs?" he asks.

I shake my head. He rushes out, then turns on his heels and comes back into the kitchen. He grabs an apple from a basket of them on the table. The screen door slams again.

I sit at the table and down the last of the cold coffee from breakfast. An apple seems like a good idea. I slice one up with my pocket knife. Then the drowse comes over me again, but I resist. I've been entirely too lazy lately.

After a second apple, I rummage through the larder to see if there's something I can make for supper. If we really live together, it's not fair to let Antonio do all the work.

There are the fixings for a rice and bean casserole, and flour and lard for biscuits. There are plenty of onions, a *ristra* of chilies, cheese, and spicy sausage. I decide I can make a cobbler with the three remaining apples. I can't think where I learned to do this. Maybe it's like riding a horse: you never forget how. I bring in an armload of firewood.

The afternoon passes quickly. I watch the shadows of the fence posts march across the corral. When I hear the truck coming, I check the casserole. It needs more time. I stir the embers.

Antonio strolls in grinning. He holds both hands behind his back. Standing an inch away, he puts his hands behind my neck, resting his forearms on my shoulders. He is sweaty and dirty. I expect not to like it, but it's all right. It reminds me of my father after a day's work.

"Which hand?" he asks. "Left or right?"

"Your left or mine?" I question in return.

"Yes," he replies.

I receive a chill like a pump handle in February at the base of my neck. Antonio kisses my cheek, and produces two bottles of cold beer. He pulls off the caps with an opener mounted in the window frame beside the table. He raises his bottle of

Dos Equis and clinks mine.

"You put more wood in the stove? It's hot in here," he declares.

"I'm making supper. It'll be ready pretty soon. I thought you deserve a break."

He looks like he's about to land another kiss on me: Hispanic custom, no doubt. Instead he puts his arm around my shoulders and leads me out back to the corral. We sit in two oak rockers in the shade of the rear *portalo*, sipping our beers to make them last. When they're empty, he lines them up with four other bottles against the wall. He tugs off his boots and hangs his socks over them.

"I got time for a bath?" he asks.

"I'll have to get more wood."

"No, I mean outside. We use the old water trough in summer, remember?"

"You got about a half hour," I say, going back to the hot kitchen.

I watch him from the window. He pulls off his workshirt and undershirt and works at the pump handle like it's a contest or something. When the trough is half-full, he strips out of his Levi's and peals down his longjohns. His bottom half is paler than his chest and back. He plunges down into the water, bending forward to immerse his head. He puffs out his cheeks and whistles. I shiver, despite standing at the stove. The well-water is as cold as a melting stream.

I realize he does not have a towel. I take him one from the hook beside the indoor tub. With the side of his fist he knocks out the wooden plug near the bottom of the trough. The dirty water gurgles into a sluice that carries it out to the vegetable garden.

"It's great to have the old Six back," he tells me, drying himself.

"Maybe," I say. "I don't remember much. It comes in bursts, like a swarm of bees. Did we use to have horses, Antonio?"

"In a way we still do. They were beautiful Appaloosas, though they were getting on. Mayflower's on the roof and Ferdinand is under the hood of the truck."

"I don't understand."

"I'm glad you don't remember, Six. You cried when the man came with his horse trailer to take Ferdie away. But we had bills to pay: a new tin roof and a new engine. You were glum for a month."

Antonio wraps the towel around himself and follows me inside. He stands next to me at the stove, turning himself around to toast all sides. I send him upstairs, grabbing the towel and snapping it at his behind. He laughs. I'm not sure what came over me. It just happened.

He descends just as I set the casserole on the table. He's in fresh Levi's and an old gym sweatshirt. We again bow our heads for grace. We dig in as though we'd been fasting all day. Antonio smiles with salsa dripping from his chin.

When I bring the apple cobbler from the stove rack, he is beside himself.

"Except for my Mama's *conchas*, this is my favoritest dessert. You remembered."

I don't tell him I just wanted to use up the last apples before they went soft. He clears the table and draws water for the dishes. He shoos me back outside, reminding me our agreement is that whoever cooks is released from kitchen patrol.

The sky ranges from star-speckled indigo to rose and gold outlining the mountains. I settle into the rocker and watch fireflies emerge from the garden. I feel peaceful and content—and full.

I come out of my drowse when Antonio gently sets my rocker moving with his foot.

"Maybe we better turn in, buddy. Need help?"

I shake my head.

"Think you're up to sharing the bed tonight? That loveseat is torture."

"You mean we share the same bed?"

"It's the only one we got."

"Well… I guess so… As long as you stay on your own side."

Antonio laughs. "We'll put a fence rail down the middle. But watch for splinters."

We go up to the bedroom. Antonio lights the kerosene lantern. He takes off his sweatshirt and kicks off his moccasins. He pulls down his Levi's and I see he is not wearing underwear after his bath. He climbs under the sheet completely naked. I decide to keep my longjohns on.

"Good night, Six."

"Que pases buena noche, Antonio," I reply, unsure where I'd picked up Spanish

I move to the edge of the mattress. I swear I can feel the heat from his body, though he's almost a foot away. His breathing grows shallow, but I have trouble falling and staying asleep. Each time he moves I think he is going to roll over on top of me. It is hard not to slide towards the middle of the mattress. At last I doze off. It feels as if hours have passed.

———————⊃o⊂———————

The windows brighten and a breeze comes up. I awaken on Antonio's side of the bed, spooned up against him, my arm across his chest. An inch further over, and we'd be on the floor.

I roll him onto his back. He makes a contented noise like deep purring. I slip out the other side, and realize I'm tenting the front of my longjohns. I'm glad Antonio doesn't see it.

I slip on my moccasins and a shirt, and steal downstairs, closing the bedroom door softly behind me. The wind-up clock on the sideboard points to five. I decide Antonio deserves to sleep late after all he's done for me this week. I go out to the shed and fetch more wood for the stove.

It is after six before he wanders downstairs, barefoot in just his Levi's. I set a mug of coffee on the table and serve him eggs and bacon and biscuits. There are two loaves rising in their bread pans on the stove shelf. A big kettle of water is near boiling.

"You've been busy. Thanks for letting me sleep in. It felt great to sleep in a bed again."

I serve myself and sit down opposite him. He studies me like I'm the most interesting book he's ever read. I'm sure my face is red, too, after his scrutiny of me. I can always say it's from working at the stove.

After breakfast, Antonio shows me the ropes on doing laundry. Beneath the rear portalo, he props a wooden washtub atop a stool and brings the lye soap, washboard, and the kettle of hot water. The wicker basket of dirty clothes is full. He instructs me to clamp the ringer on the edge of the horse trough. I fill it with water from the outdoor pump.

When he's rubbed a soapy item to death across the galvanized washboard, he rings it out by hand and tosses it into the trough. I rinse it in the ice-cold water and feed it through the wringer. I hang the clothes on the lines between the house and barn, propping up their sagging middles with forked poles. It is getting warm. I take my shirt off.

There are four pairs of Levi's, plus an assortment of denim and flannel workshirts, longjohns, khaki boxer shorts from our army days, T-shirts, socks, and the bed sheets. When the clotheslines are full, we take a break. Antonio's chest glistens with sweat. He wrings out the bandana he's tied around his forehead. We glance at each other now and then, but hardly a word passes between us. I'm a little embarrassed by how he looks at me, but maybe I only imagine it. The rest of the morning passes lazily. The day is warm and windy and our clothes dry quickly.

After unpinning the dried items from the wash line, I fold them and put them into the basket. Antonio gets back to the washtub and I to the water trough. I knock out the plug, draining the filmy water into the garden before refilling it.

At last I pin the final items to the line. It is well after lunch and I'm beat.

"We're good for another couple weeks, buddy," Antonio tells me. "Let's eat."

We are just about to go inside when we hear a car pull up in front. I don't want to pull a fresh shirt on over my sweaty torso, nor does Antonio. He's at least got his Levi's on. I'm still in my longjohns.

"Probably one of the guys from work," Antonio suggests. "You're OK."

A young woman in a sleek red dress and high heels, and an

older woman in a billowing flowered dress and hat come around to the back. Antonio and I freeze in our tracks.

"Mama. Benita," he calls out.

I scurry into the house to fetch my Levi's from upstairs. Our shirts all hang on the line. I hurry back down and Antonio hands me a shirt that's still damp.

"You forgot we were coming, didn't you, dear brother?"

"You boys didn't go to church."

"We had a tough week, Mama. Six had…"

"No excuse."

"Why don't you write it on the calendar so you don't forget?" Benita says.

"Six had an accident last week. He's still woozy."

"What happened?"

"Poor boy. What happened?"

"He conked his head some place. He doesn't remember."

I feel like I'm listening in on the party line.

Antonio's mother and sister barely let me get my shirt on before swooping down on me.

"Let's see."

"Did you go to Doctor Morgan?"

"You don't remember? What don't you remember?"

"Mama, let him be. Let's have our lunch."

As Antonio and I bring the kitchen table and chairs out beneath the still-shaded portalo, his Mom and Sis fetch a basket of food and a jug of lemonade with ice from their car. It is the cream-colored Hudson with burgundy trim I saw at the Sagebrush Diner.

The table is set with the least-chipped enamel plates and freshly-laundered napkins. There is a fat roasted chicken, a salad with tomatoes and onions and jalapeños, tortillas with corn and rice, and more cherry jack *empanadas*. I know where Antonio learned to make them.

Benita is quite a looker—like her brother. Her hair is as dark and glistening as his. They also share the trait of dimples. Mama has given her children her good looks, but she covers over her own with too much makeup. She catches me staring at her daughter.

I ask about the gleaming Hudson. Antonio taps the side of his head, explaining that I'd forgotten a couple things. He tells me the 1947 Commodore convertible had been his father's most cherished possession. He washed and waxed it weekly, and built a garage to protect it from the sun and weather. He was killed at work when a truckload of lumber slipped off its bed and crushed him. The Hudson went to Antonio's Mama, who permits Benita to drive her around in it, but forbids her to use it for her own errands. Benita's boyfriend is not even allowed to look at it.

It is a friendly gathering with plenty of laughter. I'm happy Antonio and I get a break from cooking. When the sun creeps up to the edge of the table, Mama announces they are going home. Benita packs up the basket. She gives me a hug, and a kiss on the cheek. Mama enfolds me, overlooking Antonio. She wears too much perfume.

"You take care of him," she tells Antonio. "I love you both. And next Sunday you boys go to mass two times."

She gives me and then Antonio a kiss, and crosses the side of the house to the car. She tightens the bow on her hat and tells Benita she may drive now. Benita winks at me from the sideview mirror. They drive too slow to kick up a single mote of dust.

We set the dirty dishes in a pan of water at the sink and haul the basket full of clean clothes upstairs, each of us grabbing one of the handles. After putting the fresh linens on the bed, we take off our shirts and lie down for a nap. Since we've got our blue jeans on, I don't mind if he nudges a little closer.

"I really like your sister," I say.

"She fell for you pretty hard," Antonio replies. "But I fell for you harder."

He thumps my thigh. I don't know what to say, so I close my eyes. I begin to think we are more than roommates.

———◦———

Our nap takes us almost to supper time. Neither of us is hungry, but there's an empty corner in each of our stomachs for the two *conchas* Antonio's Mama left for us. We sit out back and discuss whether or not I can work half-days next week. I decide I'm up to it.

We turn in a little before sundown. Antonio again strips down to his skin. It is still warm and the breeze has died. I decide, when it's hot at night, that it's all right if we both sleep naked—as long as he keeps a safe distance.

By morning, that distance has narrowed. The sheet is twisted in knots and we are folded around each other. It's hard to figure out which limb belongs to which one of us. Antonio is not embarrassed.

"Good morning," he says, already smiling.

We untangle ourselves and race downstairs to the out-house beside the barn. He beats me. I dance around outside until I can't hold it. I pee at the bottom of a fence post.

We get dressed upstairs and go back down to the kitchen, eating the last of Mama's chicken on a tortilla with rice. There's no time to make coffee. We head to the nursery. Nicolás has an electric hot plate in his office and his missus perks coffee for those of us who want it.

The guys slap me on the back again as if they hadn't seen me for a month. After our coffee, I drive with Mitch to a ranch with a long stretch of stone wall on each side of the driveway. It belongs to a Texan with more money than he can figure out a use for.

I am faced with piles of irregular stones harvested from the surrounding fields of sagebrush and chamisa. There are sacks of Portland cement under a tarp and a mixing trough with a hoe. As I figure out the puzzle, Mitch mixes the Portland with sand. He has to haul water from near the barn. He tosses me worn leather gloves that conform to my hands perfectly.

The puzzle seems easy enough if I don't think about how to solve it. The right stone always comes to hand. Mitch remarks that I haven't lost my touch. But when the noon hour rolls around, I'm exhausted. Mitch takes the company truck back to Mila-Grow, and Antonio swings by to drive me home for the day.

This is the pattern for the rest of the week. Antonio and I work together only rarely. Maybe this is good. We get along and

I like being around him. It doesn't bother me as much as it used to when we get ourselves into pretzel positions while sleeping. Sometimes one or both of us awakes with a boner.

"Good morning, you two," Antonio says with a sly smile.

I'm sure I must have turned the color of a poppy.

———————◦◦◦———————

A week after the Fourth of July, Antonio and I work our last Saturday until autumn. It will be a chance for us to catch up on repairs around the house and maybe paint the barn.

It is hot and dry. It looks and feels like rain, but the sky has fooled us all week. A saying of Nicolás' comes to mind from some place: *Everybody talking raining, but talking is not wet.*

Antonio and I swing by The Ornery Burro to celebrate our coming free Saturdays. We have two beers apiece instead of our usual single one. The bartender and everyone in the joint ask how I'm doing. We stay a little longer than we planned.

A clear line of dark-bellied clouds and walking rain stretches from The Gorge to The Mountain. In the rearview mirror I see the lightning flash. We can't outrun it. The wipers can't keep up. I am afraid I'll get the truck stuck in the mud a mile from home.

I credit Antonio's calmness and confidence in my driving to help us make it home. I pull up to the corral gate in clear sight of the back door. The rain lets up, but only a little. A burst of hail pelts the roof and hood of the truck.

Antonio makes a dash for it, but slides on his rear end in the mud. He attempts to get up and slips again. I can't tell which of us laughs harder.

Taking it slow in the slippery mud, I reach over and give him my hand. But instead of pulling himself up, Antonio pulls me down into the mud beside him. Two splats coat my face and hair. Antonio rolls over on top of me and pushes my backside down into the mud. My boots fill with muddy water. My Levi's weigh fifty pounds.

We roll around and rassle until we are mudmen from head

to toe. Even Antonio's smile is muddy. I pin him on his back and climb on top of him and straddle him. He squirms trying to break free, our crotches rubbing together. I slide around inside my mud-soaked Levi's.

Like a thunderbolt, I shoot my load—and shudder. Antonio smiles. I'm sure he's seen my face. I wait for his remark, but it does not come. He slides out from beneath me and hauls himself upright. He offers me his hand. I nearly slip out of his muddy grasp.

We strip at the water trough and take turns pouring icy well-water over each other's head. Antonio pumps more water into the trough as I stomp around on our clothes.

I realize the rain has stopped. A rainbow emerges above The Mountain. Antonio hangs our rinsed clothes on a fence rail and sets our boots upside down near two of the posts. Then he rinses his muddy feet at the back door. I wait for him inside with dry Levi's and a T-shirt. I rub his back with the rough towel.

We each eat two bowls of goat stew from Nicolás' missus. I want to talk about what happened in the mud, but, even more, I don't want to think about it. I'm embarrassed, but I can't deny what I felt was pleasurable.

Tonight I'm not so comfortable lying naked next to him. I put on my longjohns. It's much cooler after the cloudburst. Antonio looks at me and climbs beneath the sheet. He is a patient man.

"I had fun today," he says. "I don't have to ask if you did."

I see his smile in the dim light from the railroad lantern. I turn on my side and close my eyes.

The next morning, after mass, Antonio, his Mama, and Benita drive to a cousin's for a birthday party. Not up to a roomful of strange faces who all know me, I'm happy to be excused.

Antonio gets behind the wheel of the Hudson, his Mama next to him. She tells him which way to turn. Benita gets a break from her constant stream of advice by sitting in the back seat.

I wait for a minute in the truck, watching the other cars and trucks pull out from Santa Monica's church lot. I prayed to know what I should do, but I haven't heard. Antonio is a kind and gentle man, but I'm not sure I can ever be who he thinks I am. I drive home.

The imprints in the sun-dried mud of our wrestling match are easy to make out. Only one puddle remains. I take our dried, but now dusty, clothes from the fence. Rolling up the pair of Levi's I think are mine, I toss them onto the front seat of the pickup. I shake out the other pair and bring them upstairs. Our T-shirts and undershorts I drop in the wicker laundry basket.

I take my bedroll from the bottom of the wardrobe and pack my army duffel with items of my clothing from the dresser.

On the way out I see our work boots are nearly dry. I put mine on the floor of the truck and toss my duffel and bedroll on the front seat. My chest feels tight, like there's not enough air. I drive away before I talk myself out of going.

I pull up to the Sagebrush Diner. It's closed on Sundays so they won't know where to begin looking for me until tomorrow. I'll go back down the road the same way I wandered into Red Willow two months ago. I don't know what else to do. I leave the key on the seat.

Lacing my work boots together, I hang them around my neck. I shake out my dusty Levi's from the seat before stuffing them in my duffel. A folded piece of paper flies out of the hip pocket, stained reddish-brown with mud.

Dear Six,

I want you to know I don't ever expect you to do anything that makes you uneasy. You are the sun in my life. I'd never do anything to hurt you.

Please trust me. I will wait as long as I have to until you remember all of what we used to share, even if it takes forever. In the meantime, I can't possibly love you any more than I do.

Your Antonio

How can I leave my best friend, *mi compadre*, and just walk away from him? In the mud I learned that I have feelings for him beyond our friendship, though I'm still discovering what those are and what they mean. Two tears splatter down on the note, smearing the lines and the ink even more. I fold it and slip it back into my pocket, tossing my gear back in the truck. Maybe I need to give myself as much time as Antonio has given me.

Back at home, I carry my things upstairs and put them away. I unfold the piece of paper from my pocket and put it on the dresser where Antonio lights the old railway lantern at night. He'll know I found it. Reading the note again, I smile at how God answered me with a letter in Antonio's handwriting.

In my dream that night, I see a man in dusty Levi's and jean jacket walking across an endless field of sagebrush towards a large pile of rocks. Though I can see the figure only from behind, I know it is me.

I climb the cairn until I stand on the flat chunk of red sandstone at the top, ten feet above the ground, wondering that I have not seen the pile of stones in this field before. I shield my eyes from the last sharp rays of the setting sun, brilliant red from the clouds of dust the wind has kicked up.

From the clear sky above descends a narrow streak of lightning that strikes the man at the back of his head, blasting off his hat and knocking me to the ground.

I awaken with a start. I hold onto Antonio, enjoying his warmth, wondering whether my dream is a true memory or just a dream.

SHOOT ME, JESUS

"Please, dear Jesus, just shoot me," I thought.

Or was it a prayer? Probably not a good prayer. Or, worse, had I said it out loud?

I loosened my tie and looked around the church. The sun had not yet risen. The windows looked like pieces of darkness polished and bolted together. There was some activity in the sacristy as two altar boys in their street clothes scurried back and forth. The two candles they'd lit on the altar didn't offer much light back where I sat.

I occupied our usual place in the next-to-last pew. Antonio and I never took the last pew. According to the Gospel, the last would be first, and we didn't want to have to go first. Next-to-last was the place in church where we felt comfortable.

Now that Antonio was gone, I wondered what was the point of my going on. It hadn't been two days yet and I missed him more than I could stand. We'd worked together and lived practically our entire lives together. I was asking Jesus to take me too. Eighty was old enough.

Feeling uneasy alone in the house with Antonio's body, I'd got the neighbor girl down the road, Hermione, to drive me before dawn to Santa Monica's Church on her way to work at Walton's. Antonio and I sometimes watched her four-year-old, Adám, when her mama's sciatica kicked up. The boy was a joy. The most marvelous thing was discovering a fresh new world through his eyes. We told Hermione it wasn't ever a bother. She repaid us in cherry jack *empenadas,* which we never turned down.

I sat back in the pew and caught a couple winks. When I awoke, the first glint of daylight shone through the rose window above the altar, now draped with the funeral altar cloths of black and purple. It was the first time I'd been at church without Antonio. But he was on his way.

———————◦◦◦———————

Antonio's sister Benita had insisted on having the wake in our house, the *casita* Antonio inherited from his *abuela.* Since getting out of the army three years before Korea, it was the only place we'd ever lived. But it was not home to me any longer. Without my *compadre* around, it was only walls and floors and furniture. Now I didn't have even that.

"This house belonged to my brother," Benita told me before the mourners arrived. "Now that he's gone, you will have to leave. He did not make a will. The house is mine now. It always goes to family. You are not family, Six."

"But I am his best friend," I replied. "Even now."

"That doesn't count. It's the law: property goes to relatives. If there's anything of yours here, you better clear it out after the funeral tomorrow. I have tenants that will be moving in next week."

I was not stunned by this. Benita, who once called me her "other brother," had grown cold toward us the last couple of years, even before Antonio took sick. It was not long after the Red Willow County assessor sent a notice of our property's value—not the tumbledown house we struggled to keep in repair—but the five acres on which it stood. There were so many zeroes the number nearly rolled out of our heads. Benita's mouth hung open, and nothing pleasant or comforting has come out of it since.

The undertaker had laid Antonio out on our poor sofa. Its springs were sprung and the cushions sunk nearly to the floor. He was a little long for it. We'd always napped on the bed upstairs. He looked so uncomfortable. And cold. I complained to Benita.

"It's been our family custom for two hundred years," she told me. "If it'll make you feel better, I'll bring a blanket from upstairs."

"He liked the Hopi one."

It was probably Benita's first time in our bedroom. Either she didn't care what Antonio liked or else she didn't know one tribe's work from another's. She brought the blanket from the Pendleton tribe.

"There's only one bed up there," she said.

"Yes, we shared it."

"How cozy," she snapped.

"Yes, it was, especially in winter."

She ignored my remark and stretched the wool blanket over him. She folded his hands on top of it.

"His hands were always cold," I told her.

"Then you arrange him. I'm waiting for the aunties with their goodies."

She went out the door to the parlor and stood on the front porch. I'd always found her quite attractive, sharing traits with her older brother. But her silhouette revealed how she had allowed herself to go from ravishing to roly-poly one *concha* at a time.

It was almost sunset, the last strands of rose and gold outlining The Mountain. Above, it was deep indigo speckled with stars, like the lid of a God-size enamel coffee pot.

Only a day earlier, Antonio called me to his side, reaching for my hand.

"Better say *adios, mi compadre.* I'm on my way out the door."

I'd no sooner leaned over him, putting my lips to his mouth, than he breathed his last. His eyes were already closed, his lips curved in the sly smile he continued to wear in death.

Now, at his wake, I did not want to touch Antonio again. But his hands would be warmer under the blanket. Though less stiff than earlier, he still seemed made of wood with a coating of wax. It was hard not to break down.

The complement of aunties arrived with their platters of food. Tia Maria, Tia Leonora… I recognized them all. As soon as they whisked the food into the kitchen, they returned to lay their heads on my shoulder and weep. I had been good before that.

I lost my self-control and had to go out back to where

Antonio and I used to sit at night and watch the sky swirl around us. Another car pulled up and parked outside the corral gate, someone who knew company comes around the back. I wiped my eyes on my jacket cuffs.

It was Phineas, a guy Antonio and I used to work with at Mila-Grow Nursery. He was a skinny fellow, a few years younger than we were. Antonio joked that you could throw a handful of corn at him and miss. He was now the only one of our crew left besides me.

Phineas carried a cold six-pack of Dos Equis. He wrangled two cans from their plastic rings and popped their tabs. We clunked our cans together and took a long draught for Antonio.

Putting his hand on my shoulder, Phineas looked in my eyes. His own brimmed with tears but none escaped. He said not a word, and I knew exactly what he meant. We sat down in the pair of wooden rockers under the *portalo*. I shut my eyes for a minute. The smell of sagebrush and piñon floated on the evening breeze.

I did not return inside. Phineas, not brave enough to go see Antonio, said "Good night, Six." He took the unopened beers with him. Benita and the other mourners left, taking with them the leftover food. I was glad to be alone again, though I did not want to be by myself with Antonio's body. So I went to church early.

I awoke at the back of the church after more than just a couple of winks. The two altar boys, now in their vestments, lifted the lid of the censer and spooned more incense on top of the glowing charcoal. I smiled, knowing what fascination smoke and fire hold for ten-year-old boys.

The fragrant smoke rose and twisted and tumbled, reaching even the back of the church. The smell of lemon oil used to polish the pews and woodwork mingled with it. I decided that mixture of aromas was what peacefulness smelled like, and maybe heaven, too.

A bier draped in black waited behind me in the vestibule, ready to bear its load. The sunlight streaming through the windows scattered colored patches around the church. A dozen people now sat in the pews. The remaining candles on the altar had been lit.

Father McLarkin, who knew I called him Father Malarkey behind his back, strode to the back of the church. His cassock flapped around his ankles. I stood with difficulty as he approached, hooking my cane on the back of the pew in front. He rested his hand on my shoulder and, like Phineas, he said nothing. His sorrow, too, shone in his eyes.

Father Malarkey gestured to the altar boys and Sister Lucinda what to do next. The organist practiced a reedy hymn. Closing my eyes, I floated up with the music, and the incense, and my prayer to Jesus to please shoot me right then and there.

I awoke with a start. Never had I seen the church so full. I recited the Lord's Prayer. The words rolled off my lips automatically while the real praying was going on inside.

"Dear Jesus, I'm sorry," I thought. "How can I be so thickheaded, especially here in your house?"

I stood up, latched onto my cane, and stepped out of the pew. Walking to where Benita sat with the rest of her immediate family in the first pew, I turned and bowed to her.

"What're you doing, Six? Have you lost your mind?" she said in a whisper that could've been heard on the steps outside.

"I've come to forgive you," I told her.

"For what? I haven't done anything."

"I forgive you for being lying and greedy, for taking my half of the house. I didn't want to live there without Antonio around anyhow. Good-bye, Benita."

She puffed up her cheeks and shot out her lips as though to deliver a long, slow volley of nastiness, but nothing came out. I bowed and turned away.

I made it back to my pew just as the organ roared the processional "Saint Patrick's Breastplate." The people stood. I didn't feel so good and sat down.

I bind unto myself today
The virtues of the star lit heaven,
The glorious sun's life giving ray,
The whiteness of the moon at even,
The flashing of the lightning free,
The whirling wind's tempestuous shocks,
The stable earth, the deep salt sea
Around the old eternal rocks.

It was a hard piece to follow, much less sing. I hauled myself upright about the time everyone sat down again.

Though there was no breeze, the flag started slipping from Antonio's polished wooden casket. The lid opened up.

"Careful, Antonio," I hollered. "The flag's going to wind up on the floor."

I traversed the length of the nave before even a corner of Old Glory touched the ground. I hadn't moved that fast in years. No one paid me any mind. Antonio sat up in the casket and, swinging a leg over the side, climbed out and stood before me. He wasn't the old Antonio but the restored one, the one from when we first moved into his *abuela's* house nearly sixty years ago. He was incredibly handsome, shining. I didn't know what to say.

"I thought you were dead."

"I am, but now so are you."

"Whad'ya mean? I'm at your funeral. They played the hymn you wanted, Antonio."

"I heard. Look back at yourself," he said, cocking his head.

I turned and saw myself, looking fast asleep, eyes clamped shut. *Checking for leaks*, Antonio used to say.

"I still say that, Six. Jesus answered your prayer."

"What? To shoot me?"

"Close enough: a heart attack, quick and easy, fast as a bullet. Died in your sleep, right there in the penultimate pew. We can be together again."

"There's a two-bit word if I ever heard one," I said.

"Thank you for forgiving Benita. It's what Jesus wanted

you to do. That's what I wanted you to do, Six."

"Well, I did it anyway," I said.

Antonio laughed and I shushed him.

"They can't hear us. We're dead, remember?"

"It's confusing walking around in my restored self from when I was twenty while looking at my old self back there. Let's stay for the rest of mass."

Antonio and I walked to the last pew, still unoccupied, and sat next to each other. I put my hand on top of his. He'd warmed up nicely.

After the Communion, Antonio told me something he wasn't supposed to tell me.

"They don't like it when I peek at the future, but we're both going to be saints, Six: the Roman Catholic Church's first gay saints."

"You know I don't care for that word. Are you serious?"

"Would you rather *holy homos*?"

"Saints? How about that?" I remarked. "What'll they call us? We're not martyrs or doctors of the Church or anything."

"They will call us Saints Antonio and Sixtus, Blesséd Friends."

"That we were... are. But Sixtus?"

"The Church likes anything Latin. It sounds official. Don't forget, it's people doing this naming and sanctifying. We're all a little crazy. But sainthood comes with obligations, rarely pleasant. Little Adám there in front of us is going to develop cystic fibrosis in a couple years."

"No, sweet Jesus. Take me instead."

"He already has. But Adám's Mama will tell him to pray to his Uncle Six to please ask Jesus to spare him for his Mama's sake. You manage to wangle that favor, that miracle, out of The Man Upstairs. Adám gets cured. That gets people talking and praying. Word gets around. First you, then me. We're gonna have lots to do. You're gonna have to pray your ass off."

"I already did," I said.

"You're gonna have to sit with Adám through all the doctors and hospitals, clinics and technicians, diagnoses and prognoses, praying for him all the time."

"Will he be able to see me next to him?"

"No, but he'll know you're there."

Little Adám, on the pew next to my corpse, patted my hand.

"Wake up, Uncle Six."

The boy's mother looked over at him. I hadn't expected Hermione to come to the funeral, too, since she'd come to the wake last night. She discovered she cannot wake me. Poor girl. I would have liked to spare her that.

After the Blessing and Dismissal, the ushers rolled Antonio's casket to the vestibule. The congregation rose and passed down the nave. They paused in front of me—my corpse—and bent forward to say a few words or touch my shoulder. I just stared straight ahead like a stuffed owl.

The mourners touched or kissed the flag on Antonio's casket. When the last of them had gone out, two of the ushers folded the flag properly into a three-cornered hat and handed it to Benita.

"I see you gave my old railroad lantern to Adám," Antonio remarked. "That's good. He will shine his light every place he goes."

"That lantern's the only thing I took from the house. I wanted to leave our house to Hermione and little Adám like we discussed, but Benita snatched it. Could you talk to her? Or maybe a ghostly appearance around midnight might do the trick."

"Her change of heart will be my miracle to plead for. She's my sister. Don't worry"

Antonio and I stepped out of the pew.

"You ready, buddy?" he asked.

"Yeah, I guess I'm ready. I love you Antonio. I always had trouble saying it with words."

Antonio leaned into my ear. I thought for a second he was going to kiss me. *Not in church*, I was ready to tell him.

"I know you did, Six. I never doubted your love. And one other thing before we head Upstairs," he said in a low voice. "On the cross at Golgotha, Jesus didn't say, *Heavenly Father, forgive those here assembled.* He said simply, *Forgive* them, *Heavenly Father.* At the time, his arms were stretched wide, a gesture that means everyone, everything, the whole world. *Forgive them, Heavenly Father, for they know not what they do.* That always sounded right to me. I never met anyone who knew what he was doing."

We smiled at each other. He had never looked more handsome.

"You heard none of this from me," Antonio whispered conspiratorially. "I learned that in the end everybody makes it. Some it takes nearly all the powers of Heaven to rescue, but everyone squeaks through."

"Thank God," I said. "This sinner feels a little less like a fraud now."

We followed his casket out of the church, but did not descend the steps after the pallbearers. We continued straight ahead, floating above the stone steps.

It was getting so bright. I could barely see where I was going. I reached for Antonio's hand.

LIGHT AND DARK

We watched the storm approach from a long way off. It was west of The Gorge, maybe ten miles. At our backs, towards The Mountain, the sun still shone. First the white clouds marched toward us, thickening and growing darker. They gathered in swirling clots, curdling like milk. Their bellies turned black and ponderous. Then came the slanting rain like an intaglio of sky and, at the bottom, a distant rumbling felt more than heard.

My boyfriend, with the unlikely name of Six, never met a thunderstorm or cloudburst he didn't like. He'd make an unsurpassable Lear. As the grumbling sky began its pyrotechnic display, we hurried back down the trail to the parking lot. As the rain pelted us, I headed to the warmth and grounded safety of Six's truck. Six handed me his flannel shirt and stood at the edge of the pavement overlooking a steep ravine. I watched him from the rearview mirror. My smudged mascara and damp hair made me look like a button-eyed rag doll.

I shivered watching the rain stream down his chest in cold rivulets. I knew they were cold because the drops hit as hard as hail on the roof and hood of his pickup. Soon his jeans and boots were soaked with icy rainwater. I pulled his shirt tighter around me.

Six has been doing this for the five years we've been living together. I never thought to question it. Standing in thunderstorms seemed as much a part of him as his auburn hair and sly dimples. It gave him simple, inexpensive pleasure and it was so much fun warming his bones in bed when we got home.

Six looked skyward and raised his arms to the first streaks of heavy rain. He danced along the edge of the precipice and spouted water like a fountain, a sign he knew I was watching him. The frequency and nearness of the thunderclaps worried me, but how many dozens of times had Six done this? I'd lost count. I grew tired of his joke about my buying a New Mexico lottery ticket if lightning ever does strike him.

As I watched him romp in the downpour, my entire field of vision exploded with a white light as hot as an incandescent bulb. The crack deafened me. Snaking branches of fire seared the asphalt. I could smell the melted tar. Six was gone.

I jumped from the cab of his pickup, not considering there may still be danger. He lay where he had stood. His left boot smoldered. The copper rivets and zinc buttons of his Levi's had been yanked from the tough denim. A patch of his hair had been singed. I reviewed what little I might remember of CPR.

As I leaned down toward him, Six sat bolt upright. His eyes flashed open.

"Wow," he said. "I have seen the light."

I knew he expected me to laugh. He already had a nasty wound on the top of his head or I might have clobbered him. I helped him to his feet. His jeans were in tatters.

He was wobbly and leaned on me for support. He needed a boost to climb into his own truck. I put his dry shirt over his shoulders and made him lie against me. I cranked up the heat.

"Keep talking," I told him, something it wasn't difficult to persuade him to do. I drove as fast as I ever have in my life, and chose to swerve around potholes rather than plow through them as I usually did.

I loved Six more than my life, something I never quite managed to express to him in words. For that matter, I hadn't told myself until now.

He turned his head to look up at me.

"Yes, I know," he said. "You are my life, too."

I was unable to sit still in the ER waiting room. Their magazines annoyed me, especially *Vapid Magazine—Where Everything That Doesn't Matter Matters™*. I ripped it in half and threw it in the trash, considering it a community service. I emptied their coffee machine one cup at a time and wore a shiny path in the carpet. I pestered every nurse and attendant with questions. They should have done themselves a favor and given me a sedative.

Replaying every scene from the trailhead parking lot to the emergency room, I kept stumbling over the remark Six made that suggested he'd read my mind. He was rather sensitive for a guy, so maybe it was nothing more than his customary attentiveness. But it struck me nevertheless as a little creepy. His timing had been perfect.

Six claimed to remember little of his life before age ten, when he was taken into a foster home with five other children. He was nicknamed "Number Six," and it stuck. He told no one what his birth family's name was. After leaving his foster family at eighteen, he'd always worked for a landscaper called Mila-Grow Nursery & Greenhouse here in Red Willow. He liked his job and was good friends with two of his co-workers, Mitch and Antonio. He even got along with his boss. Everyone loved Six, especially me.

At last I settled into recalling our happy times of the last five years. Though not in a big way, marriage was on my mind the past few months. I imagined various scenarios for Six's proposing to me, from endearing to silly.

When the doctor emerged from the surgery, I'd fallen sound asleep sprawled on the hideous lounge sofa, worse than anything in my college dorm. It was nearly two in the morning.

"Hypatia Diggs?" he asked.

It was a safe bet it was me since I was the only person in the waiting room.

"I'm happy to tell you Six is going to be fine," Doctor Morgan said. "There was actually very little we could do for him. We dressed the wound on his foot. He will lose all the toenails, but they should grow back. The wound on his skull, while theoretically more serious, was even less amenable to treatment. The lightning bored a hole through his cranium and traveled an unknown route through his body before exiting through his left foot. The hole in the bone will probably not heal, but the scalp will close over it in time. He's a young man and should recover completely. But we need to keep him under observation for several days. Lightning is a strange force with unpredictable results. The full damage may not be apparent for months. Do you have any questions for me?"

"Not until after I get home," I told him. "Can I see him now?"

"I'm afraid you'll have to wait until tomorrow to see him. He's heavily sedated. Please contact my office if any questions arise. You'll be instructed on how to dress his wounds."

"Thank you, Doctor."

"Please give the attendant Six's surname. We need it for our records."

"Six is it, Doctor Morgan. That's all he's got."

"Very strange," he remarked, and turned away.

I left the waiting room disappointed at not being allowed to see Six. I'd had enough caffeine to raise the dead and was too jittery to think of going home to bed. The last place open at that hour was The Ornery Burro, way up on the north end of the Paseo.

I ordered a bourbon and soda, my calming influence whenever I was frazzled, a trick I'd learned from my father. Usually, one was all I needed, but tonight I could've stood a second. The bar was closing, though Red Willow liquor ordinance was seldom enforced. I decided I'd go home, make a ginger tea, have a hot shower, and crawl into bed.

Something seemed out of place in the house. Though I'd inherited the casita from my parents and lived in it my entire life except for college, it was not complete without Six bouncing around in it someplace. My face in the mirror drooped; my blonde hair looked stringy and unkempt. My white blouse was wrinkled and the shoulder blood-stained.

By the time I made it to bed I was so delirious I was on the verge of praying, something I tried never to do. My parents were hardly believers in the standard variety of slash-and-burn Christianity, but I couldn't believe in any God except my own, and She was not speaking to me just then.

Each time I closed my eyes I saw an after-image of the lightning flash, following the path of the veins in my eyelids. I have no idea when I finally attained sleep, but when I awoke, it was nearly the crack of noon.

I put on my jeans and sneakers, dropped on the floor the night before, and took a clean but wrinkled blouse from the laundry basket. I dashed out the door. As I reached my car, an old turquoise pickup pulled up. Antonio, Six's co-worker at the tree nursery, stepped out. He waved me over. Six sat on the passenger side, dressed for work and, in fact, already dirty. He could stand, but was unsteady. He must somehow have got home early in the morning for his clothes. He'd probably thumbed a ride.

Antonio and I got Six into the house and onto the bed. He helped me tug Six's boots off, including the left one, without laces, over his bandaged foot. I learned Six had turned up for work at the usual time. No one knew anything about his lightning accident, but they knew he was not himself. He nearly passed out twice, but would not allow anyone to take him to the hospital. He calmed down only when they told Six they would take him home to his "sweetie."

I pulled a blanket from the closet and covered Six. Then I lowered the blinds and motioned to Antonio to follow me out.

Six remained at home the rest of the week, spending most of that time in bed. Dr. Morgan said it was normal. I'd no sooner gotten off the phone than another trivially important question occurred to me and I called him back. I knew he regarded me as a pest, but I couldn't help it.

Six was affectionate and aloof at the same time. He expressed no interest in sex and I didn't push it, but every time I awoke in the night or rolled over, he had an enormous hard-on that tented the bedsheet. I couldn't wait for him to get better.

The other peculiar, and annoying, change the lightning wrought in Six was that he became maddeningly literal. It was as though every idiom, expression, and colloquialism—of which

English has a few—had been erased from his memory.

"Six, please shut your trap," I urged him when his chattiness got on my nerves. His expression was both hurt and puzzled. I had to find a work-around he'd understand. "Please keep quiet, Six."

When I told him, "See you in the morning," he informed me it was not guaranteed that we would both make it through the night.

"Thanks for that cheerful reminder."

"I do not say it to be cheerful or uncheerful, Hypatia. It is just a fact."

I switched off the light. "Good night, Six."

"I hope so," he said, "but I'll probably sleep through most of it."

It was slow at Lily of the Alley, the antique shop where I worked part-time, giving me way too much time for thought. Six no longer seemed the man with whom I'd shared my life this past twentieth of a century. The changes in him seemed big as mountains. I was sorry I hadn't protested his standing in thunderstorms like a human lightning rod long before the accident.

Six no longer wore any clothing with metal in it—no zippers, buttons, buckles, or rivets. They became hot whenever he got agitated, and either burned his skin or set his jeans on fire. I modified his favorite Levi's with Velcro and found him boots without a metal shank. It was worse than what I imagined it would be like having an infant around the house.

I was grateful when his boss agreed to let him work half-days at the tree nursery, giving Six any jobs not involving steel or barbed-wire. He became their resident expert on wooden fences, raised planting beds, and stone walkways. I owed his buddy Antonio, too, for urging Six to get up and get moving.

Six's literalness got him in trouble at work, too. We were afraid he might even be fired. It was a real-life enactment of an age-old joke.

Six was putting up a split-rail fence for a corral at a customer's hacienda out on the Mesa. A Texas tourist with a wide-assed pickup pulled over on the side of the gravel road. He wanted to cut across the corral to gather wild flowers for his wife.

"Go right ahead," Six told him. "The horses are in the pasture."

"I ain't worried about horses, pardner. I'm from Texas. What about your dog? Does he bite?"

"Nope," Six told him. "Argus is pretty friendly."

The Texan no sooner had his leg over the top rail than the dog jumped up at him, grabbed his ankle, and pulled him down to the ground. He scrambled through the fence with the dog still attached to his boot. He managed to kick the dog off, but the German shepherd made off with the heel of his fancy tooled boot.

I pictured Six's startled innocence, his dimples suggesting he wasn't entirely innocent.

"I thought you said your dog doesn't bite, you asshole."

"He doesn't, mister. But that's not my dog."

The Texan was a rootin'-tootin' Teuton with no sense of humor. He reported the incident to Red Willow County Sheriff Warren Pease, who drove out to investigate.

"I got a complaint your dog bit some rich Texan and he's pretty worked up. Came limping into my office cussing in German, that's how mad he was. He lost a boot, like as he'd rather lose a testicle. I'm afraid I'm gonna have to impound your pooch."

"Argus is at home, Sheriff. It's Hypatia's day off and she was going to take him to the river, but maybe she didn't."

"Then who the hell's dog nailed the Texan?"

"I don't know, Sheriff. That dog was hanging around all morning."

"Maybe the dog belongs to the owner of this here spread?"

"Doubt it. He took his dog Charlie quail hunting up on the ridge. Won't be back until tonight."

"Well, I got my eye on you now, Six. Better toe the line."

Six told me Sheriff Pease, thoroughly confused by the incident, left holding his hat and scratching his head. The Sheriff probably got a couple splinters.

———————○———————

Evenings after work, Six went over to Antonio's place for a couple beers and conversation, and maybe a game of cards. Sometimes he stayed for supper. He worked with this guy all day. Wasn't that enough? Was it Antonio's fantasy to seduce a straight man? Was Six's turning gay a result of the lightning? I phoned Dr. Morgan.

"No, Hypatia, dear," he told me. "It's not lightning that turns people gay. It's rainbows that make you gay."

And with that he hung up the phone on me.

I guessed I'd have to confront Six about what was going on. I'd never known him to tell so much as a white lie. I decided to get right down to it that night over supper.

"Six, have you ever kissed Antonio?"

He nodded while chewing his tamale.

"Did you like it?"

"It was OK. About like kissing one of my brothers good night."

"How many times did you and Antonio make out?"

"Just that once."

"And when was that? Last week, right?"

Six laughed, almost choking on his mouthful.

"No, Hypatia. It was a long time ago, when we were teenagers—way before I met you."

"So why do you spend so much time over there?"

"I like him. Antonio is my friend."

"So, what am I, Six?" I knew the chopped liver remark would only confuse him.

"You are my very special friend, Hypatia."

He smiled at me, dimples on high, and I was struck speechless. At last I let him get another bite into his mouth. I felt a little bit ashamed of myself.

———————○———————

Six's interest in sex had flagged so dramatically after the accident, I thought of contacting Dr. Morgan yet again. But I knew he'd only repeat his mantra of giving Six time to recover. If I complained to the doctor how horny I was, I'd only convince him I was a selfish bitch. He'd tell me to satisfy myself. But when I did, it felt as much like cheating as if I'd rendezvoused with another man at a backroads motel. Six had become my life. I'd learn to be patient until he was healed—and consoled myself with gourmet ice cream and thoughts of an engagement ring. I made up a last name for us.

My tolerant attitude changed when, about to shower, I caught Six masturbating. He, too, was naked. In his right hand he held a nail file in the electric outlet. The lights dimmed when he saw me. Little tendrils of blue lightning crackled across his skin, and all his hair stood on end. His eyes rolled back in his head. I knew better than to touch him. The noise he made was like a coyote's yowl.

"So that's why you have no time for me, you selfish bastard."

"No, Hypatia, I am protecting you. The lightning has made me very powerful."

"You gave up on me without giving it a try? How about if I tell you if it's too much?"

"All right, Hypatia. My teacher tells me this would be the safest time to engage in sex with another person."

"Your teacher?"

"Yes. I met him at Antonio's. He's a shaman. The old man says when I have just satisfied myself my energy will be lower and I won't burn you."

"Nice to know our love life is being discussed by strangers."

"Hypatia, please shut your trap."

Six lifted me up, cradling me in his arms, and carried me to the bedroom. His skin was very warm, but he was not sweating. He laid me down so gently it was like floating onto the bed. He kneeled down over me and caressed every square inch of my skin, starting with my breasts. At times it felt like he had more than two hands. There was a definite undulating electricity coming from his fingertips, but it was pleasurable, not painful, though it was always on the edge of pain. He had lit my fuse. I was ready to explode then and there.

With both hands at the small of my back, he lifted me up until he had penetrated me. My head hung backwards over my shoulders and my feet dangled off the edge of the bed. It was the perfect posture for an ecstasy, and nothing I had ever had with any man, including Six, equaled those long, slow minutes. I'd grown hoarse from moaning and hollering. After my second orgasm, I didn't care. He could finish me off anytime. I was ready to die.

Then I received a jolt from his penis that crossed the border deep into pain. It radiated outward like a black tsunami, engulfing every pleasurable sensation I had just had, negating them by waking me from the dream. I could not gather enough breath to scream. At last Six looked deeper into my eyes and saw what was happening.

He lowered me back onto the bed, gathered me in his arms once more, and carried me to the shower. The water was ice-cold, but still it hissed and sputtered on his skin. What looked like a tiny geyser shot from the top of his head where the lightning had pierced his skull. I felt the sting of the water around my vagina and knew I'd been burned. I can't say Six hadn't warned me. At least I was no longer horny.

Six helped me into a cotton nightgown and pulled back the covers. I lay against the stack of pillows he'd propped behind me. He brought me ointment from the bathroom. I reached into the night table drawer for a contraband cigarette. Rather than commencing a lecture, Six leaned over and lit it with his finger.

I felt pampered again, as though I were in a French movie, enjoying the after-sex cigarette. The burn proved no worse than a yeast infection and I recovered in a few days.

I'd wondered ever since Six returned home what he would do during the next thunderstorm. I knew what I would do: hide whimpering under the bed with his dog Argus. We'd had a month-long drought, not much rain and no lightning or storms. But it was now monsoon season in Red Willow and that pattern was about to change.

It was Saturday and Six was off work. The air felt thick; haze shrouded The Mountain. By early afternoon, the sun was no more than a bright patch in the pervasive cover of clouds. They grew dark, congealing, as thunder rumbled from far away. The sky took on the appearance of a watercolor, dripping and spreading and mixing, from rose to silver to black, eventually resolving into a clear storm front from the southwest. It was mesmerizing.

Not dissuaded by my lecturing and hectoring, Six slipped into his Velcroed Levi's and moccasins, and walked to the end of the long gravel driveway, about as far from the house as one could go without standing in the middle of the county road. He turned around to look for me.

I came up to him and wrapped my arms around his chest, facing the storm with him.

"I'm staying with you this time, Six."

"No, you're not, Hypatia."

A crack of thunder and a flash of light brilliant enough to read with my eyes closed, exploded over our heads. A pelting rain descended on us.

"All right," I told him. "Next time."

"Thank you, Hypatia."

I couldn't imagine the impossible odds that he'd get struck twice by lightning. I pulled my nylon jacket over my head and high-tailed it back to the *portalo*, where I watched Six and the storm grapple in the deepening dark. Part of me—most of me— did not believe what she was seeing. I felt unplugged from reality.

Six raised his arms to the black-bellied cloud above us. From each of his fingers a tendril of light rose skyward, thickening and branching like a river engorged with a flood of fire. When it reached the cloud, the sky responded in kind, sending the tines of a hellish pitchfork to the ground all around Six. My breath caught in my throat as gravel and dirt spat upward, the lightning creating little craters and setting a patch of sagebrush ablaze. If not for the torrent, the entire field might have caught fire. Six responded even more ferociously. In a thunderous song of answering back and forth, they did battle, two titans fighting for primacy.

At the next flash from Six's hands, the notion occurred to me that he was like the Norse god Thor and, if not a god himself, at least a son of Thor. From that thought sprang the idea that his family name, and mine, ought to be—Thorson. Six Thorson. I couldn't wait to tell him what his name was, provided he emerged the victor.

Their fury finally spent, Six put down his arms and the storm moved on, trailing tendrils of a watercolor sunset. He returned to the house and I helped him out of his wet jeans, his little friend coming to attention at my efforts. That Six had any energy left astounded me.

"This would be a good time for us to make love, Hypatia."

I looked at him questioningly. *Once burned*, I thought.

"I understand," he said, and put his arm around me. "I will be careful. I will not get carried away, as they say."

He smiled, and led me by the hand to the bedroom. Big, bad Argus crawled from under the bed to greet us, drumming our knees with his tail, as though thanking us for making the bad noises stop. I dropped my clothes at the foot of the bed.

Six had only to touch me than the tingling began, soothing and pleasurable like a warm shower or a massage. Slowly he cranked up the voltmeter, whether mine or his—or maybe both— I couldn't tell. I wanted more, then more, as though all memory and fear had vanished. By the time he entered me, I was already on the edge of the cliff. His first gentle push sent me right over the precipice. I screamed all the way down.

Thinking he had hurt me, Six withdrew immediately. I reached up to smooth the wrinkles in his forehead. He leaned on one elbow and then lay down beside me. By the time I pulled up the covers and leaned towards him, resting my hand on his chest, he was breathing in the rhythm of sleep. I heard Argus' nails click on the tile floor and, with a groan, he lay down at the foot of the bed, joining the chorus of sleepers.

While life settled once more into a routine, it was not the one I was accustomed to. Six still spent too much time with his work buddies. I reminded him more than once that I wanted to meet his shaman. Of course, that word to me was synonymous with charlatan. I got the notion this guy might be the same strange bird my parents followed as their shaman, though he'd be well over a hundred by now. My name for him had been Weird Santa because he had a long white beard and dressed in a strange red jacket with white trim.

It did not suit me, either, that the only time Six could make love to me was after he'd already jerked off. I felt he was holding back on me, though I recalled what happened when he let loose. I didn't know what I wanted, but this was surely not it.

One afternoon I went to the garage to get pliers so I could pull the rivets and buttons out and make Six a new pair of Levi's. All the tools and tool cabinets at the back of the garage had been piled high in a corner, freeing a space that looked exactly like a paint-splattered artist's loft. There were paintings and watercolors everywhere. Hundreds of them, each signed with Six's new moniker—Thorson. When had he had time to do all of this?

On the top of a drying rack made of one-by-twos, were several stacks of watercolors, all cloudscapes, all the same. But as I inspected them more closely, I saw there were subtle differences, as in a movie from one frame to the next. I judged them to be pretty competent drawings, and a few were quite dramatic, nearly abstract.

As I flipped through the stacks of watercolors, the clouds morphed from one shape into another, changing color as they passed across the sun. There was no landscape, just the parade of clouds across the various palettes of sky. One sequence went from a few summery cumulus clouds to a black sky full of storm and rage. The last drawing depicted a pitchfork of lightning. The heavy paper was singed along one edge.

I heard the rumble of Six's pickup in the driveway. It was after five o'clock and he was home from work. Where had two hours flown while I pored over his watercolors? As I heard his truck door slam, I ran out the side door of the garage and raced into the kitchen. I reached the sink and filled a pot with water just as Six entered and came over for a kiss.

"I'm a little behind tonight, lovey," I told him.

"Do I have time for a beer, then?" he asked.

"Maybe two," I replied.

I watched from the kitchen window as he went into the garage. A light switched on. I thought about something quick and simple for supper, a pasta with garlic and dried tomatoes. I had to find out what was going on.

In the uncanny way in which Six had been anticipating my movements and thoughts, he walked through the kitchen door just as I was about to call him in to supper. He deprived me of the chance to barge into his "studio" to announce it was time to eat.

With the pasta dish on our plates and a couple mouthfuls in our stomachs, I confronted him. I couldn't tiptoe around this.

"Where'd you learn to create all those wonderful water-colors, Six?"

He didn't seem the least fazed that I'd found out, but, then again, the garage, which hardly ever contained a car, was never locked. He shrugged, swallowing his food in a hurry.

"Nicolás thinks that's a result of the lightning, too."

"That's him! My parents' guru! When can I meet him?"

"How about after supper? I'll call over there. He's staying with Antonio."

"Is Nicolás gay, too?"

"I don't know about that," Six said, "but he sure is a queer fellow."

Antonio's place was not the fussy and frilly house I expected a gay man to inhabit. It was simple and not cluttered with cutesy stuff. It looked like the abode a bachelor might live in: clean and tidy, but not fastidious. He had a lot of Native American pots and rugs, and old rifles mounted on the wall. He invited us into the kiva and passed a small clay pipe I suspected contained wacky weed. Both Six and I declined.

"Nicolás is on his way," Antonio told us. "How about a beer then?"

Six and I both nodded.

Antonio was a handsome bronzed mestizo with bottom-less eyes and hair so black it looked blue. He brought four beers on a tray, a dark ale from the local brewery.

When I leaned forward to pick up my glass of beer from the coffee table—made from part of an old barn door—I saw the old man sitting in the wooden chair. He was dressed in an odd red jacket with white trim. I hadn't seen him enter the room. He reached for the glass of beer and his white beard unfurled from beneath his chin, nearly touching the floor. The glass emptied from the bottom to the top as Nicolás drank—some sort of parlor trick, I was sure.

"No, it's not a trick, Hypatia. I save the foam for last, sort of like dessert."

I shook my head.

"I see," the goofy guru remarked. "You'd rather remain convinced everything that is hard to explain is simply not real. That attitude greatly disappointed your parents."

"What do you know of my parents?"

"Enough to feel confident my remark is accurate."

Six and Antonio sat up straighter, no doubt convinced there was going to be a fight. If I were a cat at that moment, I would have arched my back and hissed at all of them.

"I am here to help, child. Six came to me after the lightning strike on the advice of his friend, who has been my student for nearly two years. You may not think so, but Six has received a great blessing, one that must be used and not wasted."

"A blessing?" I asked.

Antonio took his beer and left the kiva. I heard him go outside. It was a generous gesture to leave me and Six alone with his teacher. I wanted some answers, not an audience.

"Six has received a great deal of power from the sky. He is learning how to use it, but you must be patient with him. He will share his gifts when the time is right."

"And where did he learn to draw and paint in two months, a talent that takes years to develop?" I asked Nicolás. "Six has never touched brushes and watercolors before."

"I do not know. Lightning is a mysterious power, hardly understood even by science. But you have seen his artwork so you believe in them. Six has always wanted to create watercolors. The lightning taught him how to bring beauty to the world."

"But when did you paint them?" I turned and asked Six.

"I do not sleep much," he said. "Not since the lightning entered me. I get up after you are asleep so I do not disturb you and return when I sense you are stirring in the morning."

"And what about Six jerking off before we can have sex?" I asked the old guru, or shaman, or whatever I was supposed to call him.

"Teacher will do," he said, reading my mind. "I am like Santa Nicolás, teaching people to be generous, to give themselves. That is the best gift anyone can offer."

Nicolás leaned forward and took my right hand.

"Your man loves you more than his own life. You must believe that, Hypatia, and learn to trust him. He is protecting you from his raw power, a power that can kill. You must practice patience. Nothing will bend in your direction until you learn that lesson first. And, like Alice, you must learn to believe six impossible things before breakfast."

I felt kindness and gentleness in his touch, but I also felt great resistance to everything he said. Six scooted over and grasped my left hand. Then he took Nicolás's, completing a circle.

"How can I believe events that have no logical explanation?" I asked the teacher.

"Hard to explain does not mean impossible. There's a big difference. How many things our forebears considered impossible now fill our daily lives, including the horseless carriage by which you and Six came here?"

"But how do I begin to believe in something impossible?"

"As the White Queen told Alice, 'I daresay you haven't had much practice.' You must practice, Hypatia. That is the only way any of us get better at anything."

Six closed his eyes, and then Nicolás shut his. I felt like the sighted woman in the colony of the blind, except that I'd begun to believe it might be the other way around. I closed one eye and then the other, a little at a time.

I felt the electric tingle I did whenever Six touched me, but it was also coming from his teacher who still held my other hand. I felt the gnarls and wrinkles in the old man's hand.

Wordlessly, in my mind, I asked Nicolás what his age was, since he was already ancient when my parents knew him.

I've just had my hundred-thirty-ninth birthday—again.

I wondered whether Six had also heard this. I sensed a *Yes* inside my head in his voice. It freaked me out and I pulled my hands away, breaking our connections.

"Please, dear child, practice being patient, practice for a long time. And accept some instruction from Six."

I rolled my eyes. Nicolás frowned, and went on.

"Sooner or later, each of us must take some instruction from a man, even a man we love. It is a part of life you must accept, and use it to make you better."

The sleigh bells dangling from the front door knob jangled, and Antonio walked in. Our session with Nicolás had drawn to a close.

Antonio and Six hugged their teacher. The old man embraced me and Six. Then he left—or, rather, vanished. I hadn't seen any doors open or close. *Perhaps he's gone back up the chimney*, I thought.

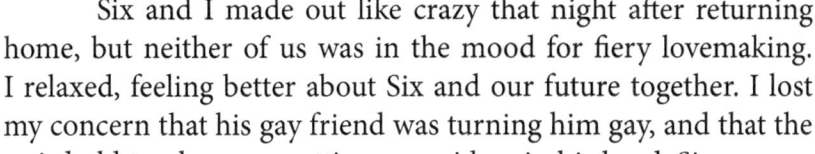

Six and I made out like crazy that night after returning home, but neither of us was in the mood for fiery lovemaking. I relaxed, feeling better about Six and our future together. I lost my concern that his gay friend was turning him gay, and that the weird old teacher was putting crazy ideas in his head. Six was capable of that entirely on his own.

When we got to bed, Six pretended to fall asleep instantly. I lulled myself with the thought that one of these days Six was going to propose to me. It seemed, if not quite impossible, at least improbable. I imagined new scenarios and found I was prepared to say "Yes" in all of them.

As I was slipping down into sleep, there was a flash. I sat instantly upright. Six had turned on his bedside lamp.

"I almost forgot," he said, sitting up and turning to me, smiling.

He placed something warm in the palm of my left hand: a ring of green stone, with beautiful banding in many shades, from pale jade to deep emerald.

"Malachite," he explained. "From an artist and jeweler in Socorro. I can't be around too much metal. You know. Will you marry me, Hypatia?"

He lifted my hand and looked into my eyes, searching them for a hint of my answer.

"I'll have to think about it, Six. It's rather sudden."

I saw his expression droop. I could no longer contain the smile waiting to burst forth.

"Yes, Six Thorson, I accept."

He placed the ring of polished stone on my finger and I leaned over to kiss him. A tiny spark shot from my lips to Six's. Or, rather, it must have been the other way around.

"If you doubt your powers, Hypatia, they will run away to find someone worthier."

"Thank you, Six," I said, and gave him another smack.

This one was stronger and made an audible crack. Six fell back against his pillow.

"That's better," he said, and switched off the light.

I managed not to sleep another wink that night, deciding who I would invite to the wedding—probably even Santa Nicolás, the Goofy Guru. Inviting him was the third impossible thing— after Six's proposal and the electric kiss—and it was hours until breakfast. Maybe it was finally time to buy a New Mexico lottery ticket, too.

ARS GRATIA ARTIST

New York City smells like a bucket of dirty mop water. The snow is clean until it touches something, then each unique flake becomes the identical dingy gray of November. Back home in Red Willow, New Mexico, snow remains dazzling until it melts. But it wasn't the climate that lured me to the Big Apple. Nor was it the attraction of fame and fortune. Quite simply, the little fish had grown cramped in his little pond and needed to flip his fins.

A cold drizzle has turned to light snow, invisible except for the nimbuses around the streetlamps. I'm looking for a quirky restaurant on Avenue A called the Café Kundalini. A friend told me it has this strange art exhibit in which the watercolors, all of clouds, morph into other shapes and colors. I don't believe him, of course, but I'd like to know what's really going on. It intrigues me. Maybe it's something I can imitate.

I see their neon sign at the end of the next block, at Eleventh Street. A windless snow squall washes everything away in a wave of white. I can barely see my gloved hand. I look behind me, no longer sure where I'm headed. My footprints have filled in; the world has fallen away. I pull up my collar and proceed, taking small steps. People rush past, featureless as ghosts, trailing swirls of snow behind them.

The Café at last appears, not by sight, but by its cloud of aromas. Even if the exhibit stinks, the meal will likely reward my traveling from way the hell uptown on Riverside Drive. I turn left, nearly smacking into their steamed-up windows. It is crowded. In the foggy glass, I see snow has frosted my sandy hair and eyebrows. I grab the brass door handle in the shape of a human hand, and the door swings open.

"Good evening, Mr. Thorson. Your table is right this way."

The maitre d' is a skinny fellow who wears a red jacket with white trim. He resembles a bad imitation of a bad Santa Claus, complete with long white chin whiskers.

"How do you know me and how'd you know I was coming?" I ask.

"You are a famous artist, sir. I have seen your picture. And if you come to a restaurant in the evening, it is likely you've come for supper. Please, have a seat. My name is Nicolás."

His explanation makes sense. I ask to see the menu.

"No need, sir. I know what you want."

"You do, huh?"

I am distracted by the snow piling up at the curb. The waiter has vanished.

A shallow oval bowl appears in front of me with two *chile rellenos*, a taste of home I'd craved for months but could not find made the right way here in New York. The waiter bows and returns to the kitchen. The *rellenos* are excellent, made properly with poblano peppers and as savory as any I'd find in dusty old Red Willow. I was missing the place more than I'd realized.

Looking up after another mouthful, I am drawn to the artwork on the walls, each one, as my friend had described, a cloudscape well-executed in watercolors. They are small, but incredibly forceful. In one, depicting an ominous anvil-shaped thunderhead, I think I see a flash of lightning. Must be a reflection from the street, except that it is still snowing, harder than ever. It looks as though someone has painted the windows white.

I return to the art. The thunderhead has moved in the frame. Its leading edge, of slanting rain and lightning, has moved into the next picture frame on the opposite side of the doorway to the kitchen. The other watercolors have changed in subtle ways, too. The Tibetan brass bell over the front door jangles. My waiter walks in and stamps his feet on the floor to shake off the snow. I did not see him go out. He looks like a Santa, albeit a weird, skinny one.

The watercolors pull me in one direction and the delicious aromas of my *rellenos* in another, each too powerfully to allow split allegiance. I nibble in between long stretches absorbed in the artwork, drawn to it and into it as though mesmerized or on some sort of drug. I wonder if there's something in the food that's making this happen.

"Certainly not, Mr. Thorson," Nicolás says, standing at my elbow. "It is powerful work, is it not?"

I nod, and glance back at the painting.

"Would you care to meet the artist, sir?"

"Is he here tonight?" I ask.

"Indeed he is, sir. Just one minute, please."

The funny little waiter turns and goes into the kitchen, emerging a moment later with a tray on which sits a red napkin. He sets the tray before me and lifts the napkin. There is a round mirror which he holds up to me. It startles me to see my face so changed. My hair is thinner and grayer. Lines at the corners of my eyes and mouth nearly connect. But my eyes are brilliant blue and piercing. I look up at Nicolás for an explanation.

"Your work is on loan to us by Six Thorson from ten years hence, from the future. That is when you will do your best work. You will stop fooling people and create from deep within you. That is why the work has such tremendous energy and does not remain static. It is alive."

"Everything is appearances," I tell him, "all on the surface, skin deep, a coat of paint, a whore's rouge. There's not much else, I'm afraid."

Nicolás scowls. I look away and consult my phone. It is nearly midnight. Where had two hours gone? My agent has sent a half-dozen frantic messages.

I pay my check and stand at the glass entrance door, dismayed by the featureless landscape, the frozen wasteland of Siberia that has descended on New York City.

"Your cab is here, Mr. Thorson."

I cower into my jacket and dash out the door. There is no snow to be seen, not one flake. The pavement is damp with drizzle and light fog. It is the city in November. I open the door of the cab and slide onto the seat.

I have a reverie all the way home, the first wisps and whispers of my next series of paintings, the very thing my agent has been exhorting me to develop for months. It will surpass my most brilliant work, "Locked Gallery." No one was admitted to the exhibit, and still the critics swooned and fawned. I wonder what makes me tilt toward Expressionism in the future. Or maybe that little display at Café Kundalini was mere artifice and not art at all.

***

My agent, Sol, is not thrilled by the concept of "Art Without Boarders," though when I mention hiring a Lesbian Hispanic crew from The Bronx to execute the work, his face brightens. He approves of inclusiveness as long as there are no white men.

"Good publicity," he says.

"You know all the promo materials have the title of the exhibit misspelled."

"Really?" Sol remarks.

"The exhibit is not advertising rooms to let. There is no 'A' in 'Borders.'"

"Well, then it neatly sidesteps any trademark infringement issues, doesn't it?"

"The man with an answer for everything. When's the world going to end, Sol?"

"When no one's looking," he replies.

"Then I'm afraid it already has."

***

"You know how nervous it makes me, Six, when we get this close to our opening and I see no indication that anything is going on," my agent says.

We stand at the center of the sixty-by-sixty foot space, made into a sixty-foot circle by means of curved panels. One sliding panel forms the doorway. Everything—walls, floor, and ceiling—are pure white.

"But it's finished, Sol, all ready for Friday night," I tell him.

"When will the paintings arrive?"

"They're here, Sol, all hung and ready to go, all of them white and featureless, as we discussed. No doubt the house painters who did the work brushed and rolled in no consistent pattern, so there are small differences of texture from panel to panel."

"But how will anyone know where the art ends and the walls, the room, begin? There are no frames, no edges, no borders," Sol complains.

"Exactly. That's the whole concept, remember?"

"Yes, but I thought there'd be some way to distinguish the individual works besides microscopic textural differences."

"There is: the placards beside each painting with title and catalogue number: *Untitled 1. Untitled 2, Untitled 3*, et cetera."

"What if a patron or collector wishes to purchase a work? What will we do?"

"Ask them where they'd like to display the art and then send The Bronx painting crew to their house with the bucket of white paint and a roller. Simple enough."

Sol has been fingering every inch of the walls looking for the panel that slides open, looking for his way out, but it's too late. He's already signed off on the whole concept of "Art Without Boarders." He has no say in the execution of my artwork.

"I don't know, Six," he says, wagging his head. "What are the critics going to say? How many times can you punk them and still have them on your side?"

"I'll let you worry about that, Sol. You're so much better at it."

I touch the tiny gray dot, the finger hole between the first and last works of art, and slide the panel open. His sigh is audible.

"I thought we'd never get out of there," Sol says. "I felt like I was lost in a blizzard."

I put my hand on his shoulder and thank him for at last getting the gist of this installation. He hasn't a clue what I mean, just as it should be.

I do not usually care what the public or critics think of my work. I haven't actually drawn or painted anything since coming to New York ten years ago. My studio is as sterile as an operating room, yet I am hailed and emulated. You can't fool anyone unless they're willing to be fooled. You can't lie to anyone who doesn't want to be lied to, and they are complicit in the lie.

This exhibit feels different, as though there were more riding on its reception than I realize. I've been unable to keep anything down since cold cereal at breakfast. My stomach is in knots. Sol is annoyingly chatty and optimistic. I send him on a fool's errand for some kosher bacon for the wrapped shrimp to get him out of my hair. I don't care when he gets back.

Over and over my thoughts return to my work of the future, the series of cloud pictures. That weird waiter played on my mind. I may return to Café Kundalini just to let him know I do not buy into his lie, or trick, or fantasy, or whatever it is. I detest Expressionism.

I pace the exhibit in circles, first one way and then, I think, the other. It's hard to tell. I am lost. I'd be even more lost without Sol. I wish I hadn't sent him away. I have an idea and the show opens in an hour.

At last I hear the freight elevator. Sol returns empty-handed. I forget what I sent him for.

"I found kosher bacon and shrimp. I took it to the caterers on the third floor," he reports.

I doubt there is any such thing, but I am not Jewish. I defer to Sol. Of far more importance is my idea.

"I want all the works in this show, each of the white spaces on the wall, to have the same title: Untitled 1. I want to give my viewers nothing. The less I show them, the more they see."

"By tonight?" Sol asks.

I nod and he is off. I know he'll get the title changes done in time. I don't know what I'd do without Sol.

I stand at the video monitor in the gallery office watching

the attendees milling about and consulting their catalogues. All of the pages look the same—white, blank. Sol looks at his clipboard and points to the screen. I know he has gotten useful tips from the doorman, who knows every B-list celebrity and higher by sight, regardless of disguises.

"Is that a nun?" I ask. "She's perfect in that black habit. A crow in the snow."

"Benedictine," Sol replies. "Sister Hildegarde von Binghamton, from Upstate New York. You may think she's taken a vow of poverty, but not Sister Hildegarde. She's a famous astronomer and makes millions off her popular books. She's a friend of the late Stephen Hawking. Her habit is silk and her high-clopper shoes custom from Gucci."

"How do you know all this, Sol?"

"It pays to know."

"Yeah, I guess. And what about the two biker dudes? More black on white. A pair of crows."

"Don't have their last names, but they are Mitch and Antonio, boyfriends, a gay couple, whatever you call it. My contact will say only that Antonio is about to come into pots of moolah from an inheritance. They can afford you."

"Good. I dislike freeloaders. They've been raiding the refreshments table like their legs are hollow, making a meal of it. And who's the fellow in the expensive suit, the fat crow?"

"It's probably a cheap suit. That's Biggs, no first name. He's actually Biggs IV, from a long line of New York robber-baron philanthropists. He's chairman and CEO of the Vorax Corporation. Easily a multi-billionaire. Rumors say he's scouting locations for a museum to bear his name and logo. Wouldn't hurt to get a work or two of yours in there, Six."

"Let's get upstairs, Sol. Stalling makes me nervous. I want to overhear what they're saying about me."

Sol continues chattering in the echoic stairwell about who else he has seen or who is rumored to be coming. I haven't a clue who most of them are. They could not interest me less as long as they continue to support me. Besides, their investment in my work has not hurt them, either.

"...and the van Burens, and a state Supreme Court judge..."

"Sol, please, enough. You lost me at the bottom of the stairs. Just stay at my elbow and remind me who they are."

We enter through the open panel. No one looks in our direction. My flowered Nehru jacket, striped trousers, reflective sunglasses, and multi-colored beads have thrown them all off the scent until I am ready to reveal myself. Another of Sol's wicked ideas for my disguise. An older couple and an even older matron rush me like I was the sale counter at Macy's.

"Mr. Thorson. Perhaps you don't remember..."

My disguise has fooled no one, it appears. Sol leans into my ear.

"Charles and Helen van Buren, Upper West Side collectors. Big-time. Own three of your works. In the company of Zelda Popper, art adviser and procurer to the stars. Be nice."

"Of course I remember you, Mrs. von Schmeltznik .Thanks for coming," I tell her.

"I'd say you were trying to insult your viewers," Zelda Popper intones. She and the pug under her arm both snuffle, and then she and her clients turn away.

Sol rushes in to save me. He takes hold of my elbow, guiding me like a tugboat through crowded waters. He whisks me to the other side of the round refreshments table.

"Dr. Egad De Bockel, world-famous Dutch-Israeli psychiatrist. Owns two of your works, from the all-black series: Nighttime in an Inkwell Nos. 1 and 2. Mention his latest book."

He rushes the doctor before I can ask him the title of the book. The doctor has a completely white head of hair and full beard. His head disappears in front of my artwork. Sol extends his hand to him and pulls me closer.

"Dr. De Bockel. Good evening. We were just discussing *We're All OK*, weren't we, Six?"

"Complete tripe," I say, "with a dash of drivel."

"I have never been so insulted," Dr. De Bockel huffs and sputters.

"Then I'd say it was about time, wouldn't you, Sol?"

The scowl on Sol's face has brought several wrinkles out of

retirement. He mouths something to me, but I do not understand. He pulls me right in front of my work, *Untitled 1.*

"What's the matter, Six? You're not yourself tonight."

"Or maybe tonight I am myself."

"Let's hope not."

I find myself next in front of the banker/industrialist Biggs IV. Despite his bulk, he is surrounded by two even beefier bodyguards in matching sharkskin suits, a pair of shiny crows.

Biggs says nothing. His eyes narrow. He turns and spits at the wall. Spittle dribbles down *Untitled 1.* The two bodyguards close behind him like steel elevator doors. Sol whirls me around.

"I was afraid this would happen," he tells me, wrinkling his forehead. "We went too far."

"I'm surprised it didn't happen a dozen exhibits ago. Remember "Painters' Strike," all empty frames and all of 'em eventually sold?"

At last my dear agent laughs.

"That's the spirit, Sol. We had a good run."

I pat him on the back and urge him toward the fellow in what looks like judicial robes. I learn he is wearing a plain black kaftan and *namaz* hat, an observant crow.

"Allow me to introduce you to Judge Basim Fastidi of the New York State Supreme Court."

He looks Middle Eastern, brown skin and dark, curly hair. We bow to each other.

"So how does a Muslim get on the Supreme Court?" I ask, guessing he's Moslem.

"By upholding the law," he replies, smiling. "How does an artist get to be famous and sought after without painting anything?"

"It is all appearances, your Honor, a coat of paint. I show the nothingness underneath, the emptiness at the heart of reality."

"Do you truly believe that, Mr. Thorson, or have your handlers taught you to say that?" he asks, glancing at Sol.

"Bingo, Judge. Now I know why you're on the Supreme Court. I'll see you around."

Sol bows to Judge Fastidi and urges me on. I recognize the next fellow. His face is plastered on every screen and billboard in

New York. He is Lance Parker, thirty-eight-year-old skateboarding champ. He introduces us to his attorney, Juan de Crisco, Esq., who accompanies him everywhere to make sure there are no infringements of his client's copyrights or trademarks. He informs me my exhibit is "clean."

"Is that so?" I say, snatching the pen from his jacket pocket. I make Lance's trademark X on the wall. He is purported to be unable to read and write, the perfect role model for the generations that emulate him. I mark each of my works with Xs, no two alike, some large, some small. There are gasps; everyone turns around to look. I hear someone ask, "Is this performance art?"

"Your people will be hearing from me in the morning, Mr. Thorson."

"Sol is the only people I've got," I tell Mr. de Crisco. "And if I fire him, there'll be no one to answer the phone."

Sol turns around to make sure I'm only kidding. He hastens off to lasso another patron. Lance Parker touches my sleeve and asks to have a word with me, out of earshot of his attorney.

"I am assumed to have oatmeal between my ears because of how I earn my living. That is Sister Hildegarde von Binghamton across from us. I read her paper on "Directional Factors Pertaining to the Gamma Ray Bursts of Wolf-Rayet Hypernovae." Perhaps that doesn't make me smart, but it does indicate I have interests outside my chosen field. What I am wondering, if you are considered such a clever artist, and your work so profound, is the opposite perhaps true? Are you, as Ezra Pound put it, a Hollow Man, Mr. Thorson?"

"I'll have to get back to you on that later, Lance, old pal," I tell him, thumping my chest.

I watch him leave the exhibit. I haven't a single friend or advocate in the entire place. They're saying, *We're not buying it*, literally and figuratively. They all hate me and they hate my work.

"Not everyone, Mr. Thorson."

It is a wiry-haired fellow in a striped shirt, the delivery guy from ESPizza. The caterer was told to call them if they were running out of finger food.

"I like your work, Mr. Thorson, though I am more impressed by the concept than the execution. I'd rather read a paragraph or two about your concept than have to actually sit, or stand, through it. Here. This one is yours."

He takes a small cardboard pizza box from the stack and hands it to me, then goes off distributing the others among the gallery attendees. I learn from Sol he is Oscar Diggs, the owner and proprietor of ESPizza. *We know what you want*™. The claim is that Oscar Diggs is a wizard who knows what toppings you want before you know it yourself. He has the steaming pizza at your door within a minute or two of your thinking about it.

My personal pizza is exactly what I was craving, topped with red and green chiles, refried beans, lots of cheddar, avocado, and black olives. Sol's pizza is marked, "Kosher. Really." It's loaded with anchovies, tuna, salmon, and enough garlic to repel every vampire in Hollywood. Judging by the reactions of the other patrons in the gallery, Mr. Diggs has scored more direct hits. Can he really read minds? I want to know if this is legit.

"Of course it is, Mr. Thorson," Oscar Diggs says, standing at my shoulder. "Mind reading is a small talent. But it makes people happy and it pays my rent. How about you?"

"I am always behind on paying my expenses despite the ridiculous amount of money I make peddling empty frames. And it does not make me happy to..."

I stop myself, wondering why I am telling this to a stranger.

Because you have no one you can confide in, Mr. Thorson. You are alone and lonely.

Diggs is talking right inside my head. I answer him back.

I am also afraid, I think at him.

Because of the new path you are setting out on?

Yes, I think. *I want to give all this up and go back home, back to New Mexico.*

"It is the right choice, Mr. Thorson," he says aloud. "You will make yourself and many other people happy. Your life will be a success."

Oscar Diggs smiles at me and, after seeing that everyone is sated, winds his way to the entrance. Now that they have been fed, a good many of the patrons of art rush out with him, just short of a stampede. The nun, the two bikers, the Muslim judge, and some scraggly fellow too thin to cast a shadow remain. Yes, and good old reliable Sol, who has promised to fire himself after tonight. He wants to move to Florida and take up miniature golf. "Gotta start small," he says.

The dark-haired biker, Antonio, asks to have a word with me.

"Did you intend the spelling as 'Art Without Boarders,' Mr. Thorson, or was it a mistake?"

Leave it to a couple of homos to know their homonyms. They laugh as though they, too, have homed in on my thoughts.

"It was a mistake," I admit. "I did not care enough about my own work to even glance at the designs being sent to the printer."

"Kind of empty and sad without boarders, don't you think?" the other biker, Mitch, asks.

I shrug, but must admit my work is rather vacant. There is certainly nothing of me in it.

"I'd like to introduce you to my cousin," blond-haired, blue-eyed Mitch says to me.

I assume he means the scrawny fellow who scribbles something in his notebook before each painting—but I was wrong.

We stand before the nun, who is drinking from two glasses of red wine: a real two-fisted drinker. I actually remember her name and preempt both Sol and the gay bikers.

"Sister Hildegarde. No, I have not read your book, I'm afraid. None of them. I flunked math and science."

"Well, that's refreshing," she says, raising both glasses to me. One is already empty. "I don't believe a single person ever told me that, Mr. Thorson."

"Does everybody in the joint know who I am?" I ask Sol. "What good are disguises? I might as well be comfortable then."

I unbutton the top of my Nehru jacket and strip off the long-haired wig. Sister Hildegarde offers another toast: *To Authenticity.*

"Care for some wine?" she asks me.

The nun pours two glasses of spring water, handing one to me. It turns a deep red. I take a sip. It is a very good merlot.

"One of my odd little talents. But at least I express it. You are hiding yours under a basket, Mr. Thorson, under layers of gimmickry and tomfoolery. I at least expected a couple of witty titles: *Sheep in the Blizzard, Blackboard Negative*. But you are stingy, stingy with yourself. Be who God made you, Mr. Thorshon," she says, sloshing her syllables, "and share yourshelf."

Sister Hildegarde refills our glasses from the bottled water, and it all turns into wine. Antonio and Mitch act as though everything is hilarious. They punch each other on the arm for emphasis. The skinny guy moseys over and introduces himself as a Goth Beat poet.

"My name is Edgar Allen Ginsberg. Perhaps you've heard of me."

I and the entire group shake our heads. I feel bad for Edgar. I may not have an ounce more talent than he does, but at least I am well-known.

There seems to be no end to the amount of wine Sister Hildegarde pours from her water bottle. The wine is strong, and I feel it coursing through my brain. The bikers are hanging on each other, less out of affection, it seems, than for steadiness. I hope they came in a cab and not on their Harleys. The poet tries inserting himself into whatever shred of conversation is initiated. The wine has loosed his tongue, too. The only clear-headed person in the room is the observant Muslim, Judge Fastidi.

As I watch, he holds up an empty glass to Sister Hildegarde, who fills it with water that quickly turns into wine. He dips two fingers in the wine and flicks the drops of wine over his shoulder before taking a sip. I ask him the meaning of this custom.

"The Holy Koran states, 'The first drops of wine shall be thine undoing.' So I discard the first drops and imbibe only those that follow."

"Here! Here!" Sister Hildegarde shouts. "The Judge remains observant—in Jesuitical fashion."

Antonio and Mitch support themselves by leaning against the wall, their elbows touching *Untitled 1*. The poet is reciting to them. I see the tiny spots and dribbles of wine from Judge Fastidi on *Untitled 1* behind him. Sister Hildegarde refills my glass. I move to the other side of the room, away from everyone, and, with a sweeping motion of my arm, splash the entire glass of merlot across several of the paintings. The room falls silent.

"I told you he was a performance artist," Mitch tells his boyfriend.

Edgar Allen Ginsberg pipes in with, "A slashed wrist is the first brushstroke of Expressionism. The purpose of life is to die."

I daub and splash at the walls as fast as Sister Hildegarde can refill my glass. She quickly gets into the spirit. It has been years since I had this much fun, maybe since coming to New York. I certainly have not felt this connected to my work since leaving Red Willow. The nun seems not to care about spilling red wine on her black habit, but the other spectators stand back.

Though I have no idea what I am creating, it feels important to me, as though I cannot turn away from what I've begun. All the white is covered. At first it looks to me like the scene of a slaughter, but then the gaudy Rorschachs seem to unfold themselves, revealing new interpretations. I face my dedicated patrons who stayed with me until the end.

They begin fading like old photographs, the color leached away by time and forgetting. They nod approvingly, but when they speak I cannot hear them. Soon they are far away, beyond the horizon, lost in the vanishing point, until I can no longer see them at all

I face the wall. My work, too, is fading, the wine reverting to water a drop at a time, and evaporating. The walls are white again. I see nothing. White, white, white, like a blizzard. My aloneness is palpable.

A hand rests on my shoulder, a bony hand. I jump, and turn around. It is the strange waiter from Café Kundalini, dressed in his red jacket with white trim. We now stand at the door to the restaurant in the East Village. He bows and, with his eyes, directs me to look outside. A true blizzard has descended on the city, a white-out, though it is not a solid white. It is real snow. I notice the texture of swirls and eddies and arabesques. The weird waiter clears his throat.

"It is said each writer has a stable of six characters. All others are variations on one of the six. You are Number Six, the artist, the creator. I am Number One, Santa Nicolás, the giver and teacher."

"And who are the others?" I ask.

"I think you know them, Six, but I shall tell you. Sister Hildegarde von Binghamton is your spiritual self, the priest, or priestess in this case. Oscar Diggs, the owner of ESPizza, is the wizard, the magician. He is Number Three. Number Four is the judge, His Honor Basim Fastidi, the part of you endowed with wisdom. Number Five are the bikers Antonio and Mitch, who are both friends and lovers. You have your own special friend back in Red Willow, Six. Remember?"

"And who is that?"

"Who else, Six? It is Hypatia."

I laugh. "I doubt she is still waiting for me, Nicolás. It's been ten years."

"Love makes us do such impossible things," the teacher says, looking into my eyes. "If you believe she has forgotten you, then that is how it will be. But I like to think Hypatia is waiting for you to return. Look. Isn't that her? Remember, it can be anybody you want, Six."

He points out the steam-shrouded door to a shadowy figure crossing Avenue A. The teacher's fingertip touches the glass and a clear dribble descends to the bottom of the door. I see it's Hypatia through that narrow sliver of clarity in the foggy glass. Nicolás opens the door and I step outside into the swirling snow. He hands me a small package, what feels like a book. I thank him, bowing, and walk towards Hypatia. A squall of snow conceals her.

I stand now on the flagstone walkway to Hypatia's house in Red Willow, the one she inherited from her parents. It's also the place I'd called home for five years—before I left for New York. She stands at the front door in a thin sweater, hugging herself. She locked herself out.

"How long have you been standing there, Hypatia? You look frozen."

"About ten years."

We laugh.

"You wouldn't still happen to have your key somewhere, would you, Six?"

I reach into the pocket of my jeans and hand her my key ring.

She opens the door and we rush into the kiva to the fireplace. I look at her, the flames dancing in her eyes, her blonde hair shimmering.

"You wouldn't still happen to have that object made of malachite I gave you before I left, would you?" I ask her, grinning.

Hypatia puts her hand into her jeans pocket and produces the polished green ring.

"Maybe it's time we put it to good use," I suggest.

She smiles. "How about tomorrow?"

"Christmas Eve? Who'd we get to officiate on such short notice?"

"My parents' old shaman, the guy I used to call 'Weird Santa' when I was a girl. He'll do, if you're not fussy. He's registered with the State of New Mexico."

I realize she must be talking about Nicolás. He's probably folded up origami-style somewhere inside my bag.

"I'm not fussy," I tell her, "except about who I decide to spend my life with."

Hypatia puts her arms around my neck and pulls me closer. She feels warmer to me than the fire. My bones ache to lie next to her.

———◦◦———

Hypatia finds me in her back garden, collecting meltwater from the icicles dangling from the portalo.

"You've opened a present early," she scolds. "'Techniques of Watercolor?'"

"Yes," I tell her. "It's from Nicolás, my teacher. He wanted me to open it as soon as I got home."

"Are you home, Six?"

"Yes," I say, giving her a kiss. "And the book suggested I collect water for the pigments from a natural source like a brook, or waterfall, or a thunderstorm. At the moment, this is the only unfrozen water in Red Willow."

We hear a clattering in the kiva, like someone coming down the chimney. We find a sooty Nicolás standing at the hearth, his grin and eyeballs the only parts still white.

"Dearly beloved," he intones, and takes hold of our hands.

Hypatia and I look at each other. Her smile lights up her face, and probably mine, too.

LESSONS ON AMERICA

Auntie Moona called to tell me Uncle Habib did not come home. She called me two hours ago, but I did not hear her knocking on the door to my room. I had my headphones on, listening to Brief Heavy Downpours, my favorite. Auntie knows her twelve-year-old nephew does not speak such good English. She asked me to go look for Uncle.

There is a curfew in the park that prohibits persons from being there between one and six in the morning. Once I step off the bridge from City Island, I am in Pelham Bay Park. It is nearly three in the morning. I could be arrested and sent away like my father. That is why I pay attention to all the laws. I do not know where they send people arrested in America. Maybe to Chicago, where they are never heard from again.

There are many stars tonight, and some lights from the city. It is easy to see where I am going. I look for Uncle's red and white and green umbrella with the yellow letters, *Habib's Halal Market*. I know he pushes his food wagon along the concrete walkway at the edge of the sand. But Orchard Beach is long and I am tired.

It is hard walking in the sand, like dreaming, walking so slow, the ground grabbing at your feet. I think I see his wagon, but it is no use hurrying. The faster I walk, the slower I go.

I love my Uncle more than anybody. He is my mother's brother. One day, he told me, when I graduate high school, he will adopt me. But I worry I will never learn English. It's too hard. Each word means so many different things and many sound alike.

I see Uncle Habib's food cart. His umbrella is down. Everything is shadows. I try to walk faster, but it feels like I am going backwards. I do not see my Uncle. I am worried he is sick.

Uncle has made a shallow pit in the sand and covered himself with his *jānamāz*, his prayer rug. It is cold at night and there is much dew on the beach.

"Uncle!" I shout. "Uncle Habib!"

"Quiet, Basim. You'll disturb the stars," Uncle whispers.

He rolls up his rug and sits up. He pats the sand and invites me to sit beside him.

"This is the only place in New York where you can see stars like back home," he tells me.

"I do not know. We were afraid to go out after dark," I remind him.

"Yes, poor boy. The stars and the moon were taken from you. But now you have them back."

Uncle Habib pats my knee. I am sitting on my hands. The sand is warm where Uncle has lain.

"I know your Auntie has sent you. But I cannot go home just yet. Stay with me, Basim."

"Yes, Uncle."

I am pleased he has asked me to stay. I do not wish to trudge back so soon, especially if we must haul the wagon.

"I have lost the money. Your Auntie will be very angry with me."

"Lost, Uncle? How? I will help you look for it. Soon it will be morning."

"Someone has taken it, my child. I was robbed."

"What did he look like, Uncle? I will find the man, beat him up, and get your money back."

"Worse is the shame, my boy. It was a woman. Two women. They came to my food wagon to order something. They spoke our language. They fluttered their eyelids at me. I was flattered. Beware of flattering women, Basim."

"I will, Uncle. I'll be very careful of women who smile."

I see my Uncle grinning. His teeth appear in the faint light, and a sparkle in one eye.

"One woman was deciding what to order and talking like a magpie. The other woman slipped behind me while I was listening to her friend and stole the cash box. Two-hundred eighty-one dollars. Auntie will be hot as a pepper."

I want to ask Uncle what the women looked like, but he is too kind and will not report them. Uncle Habib likes to tell me, *The devil always wears familiar garb.* Now I know what he means.

"You should call your Auntie, Basim. Tell her I am safe, but say not a word about the money."

"I won't," I promise him.

I reach into my pocket for my phone. I also find the envelope Uncle's friend brought me after school, tucked inside the schoolbook I had lost, my English lessons. I don't know where his friend found my book.

"This is from Mr. Nicolás," I tell him.

He crinkles the envelope and feels its thickness. I call my Auntie and tell her all is well, that I have found Uncle and will stay with him until daylight.

We lie back on the sand and Uncle Habib covers us with his *jānamāz*. I do not know if this is acceptable. But if Allah has made the night cold, and has blessed my Uncle with a beautiful rug, how could we not cover ourselves with it?

I have never seen so many stars. There are too many. As I stare up at them, the earth moves, just a little. I feel dizzy and close my eyes. I hear my Uncle snore. Even though I do not know how to pray, I thank Allah that he has kept my Uncle safe. I love my Uncle more than anyone. As much as I loved my Mother.

I awake shivering. It is near dawn. The sky ranges from fiery white at the horizon to deep blue above, but the sun is still below the water. It is Uncle's praying that awakened me. I sit up.

Uncle crouches on the rug, facing where the sun will rise. His forehead touches the rug. I do not understand much of what he is saying.

When he is finished saying his *Fajr* prayer, he rolls up his rug and crawls back to me across the sand. He pulls himself up by the handle of his food cart. Uncle sends me to the water fountain to get water for coffee and cooking. I feel the first warmth of the sun on my back.

After Uncle grinds the coffee beans and puts the water on the burner, he tears open the envelope from his friend. It is full of money. Uncle counts.

"Two-hundred eighty-one dollars," he says. "And here is a note. Read it to me, Nephew."

"Yes, Uncle Habib. This *abjadīyah*, this alphabet, I understand. It reads, *Dearest Habib, As the saying goes, you cannot steal from a thief. I believe I have recovered the correct amount from the thieves. Yours, Nicolás. PS I have no doubt your nephew will graduate English at the top of his class.*"

"I am proud of you, Basim."

"But this is not American writing, Uncle. Here. Look."

I glance down as I hand Uncle Habib the note from Mr. Nicolás. It is now all in English and I recognize every letter and I understand every word.

Uncle smiles at me as he pours too much milk and sugar into my coffee. He does not make it the American way, naked, as he says. I want to ask him how his friend knew how much money had been stolen—knew it the day before—but I know what he will tell me. He will shrug his shoulders and turn his palms up.

"Why don't you ask him?" Uncle says.

I help my Uncle open his red and white and green umbrella with the yellow letters. We lift it up and put it in the holder on the side of his food cart.

"I *will* ask him," I say. I hope I have not shown disrespect.

"The boy becomes the man," he remarks.

I promise I will go see Uncle's friend the next time I am in the village of Manhattan. I have coffee with Uncle and then head to school. I know he is watching, so I make sure to turn the right way at the painted iron bridge.

Nicolás is the new owner of Uncle's old store in the City. It is now a café. Café Kundalini. It is Indian, I think. I did not recognize Uncle's friend in his handsome red jacket. His full white beard is neatly trimmed. He bows to me and folds his hands.

"Thank you, sir, for finding my book," I tell him.

"A good man is grateful and always remembers his debts, though I suspect you hoped that book would stay lost forever."

I nod to him and look down. My face is hot.

"Come, let us have tea."

The tea pot and tea glasses appear on an empty tray in Nicolás's hands. There is a jar with honey, but no milk.

"You want to know how I know things? How I do things.?"

I nod to Uncle's friend.

"I have never learned anything without first wondering about it, Basim. There are no answers without questions."

The tea is made with rose-hips. It is my favorite. My mother made such a tea for me when I was very young. Just a sip with lots of honey, especially when I was sick.

"How did I learn American so quickly, Nicolás?"

"I read your English lessons, the whole book, kiddo, cover to cover. It was a real snooze. When you touched the book after I sent it to you, you learned everything I learned."

"But why? Who cares?"

"Your Uncle cares, Basim. Your Uncle is sick. You must become his son very soon. I have asked a lawyer to draw up papers so it can happen. Please take these with you. You and Uncle Habib and Auntie Moona must sign them."

A thick envelope appears in Nicolás's hand, and a fresh pot of tea on the table. It is a different tea, more like the dark tea my Uncle makes. We touch glasses and smile.

I think that the picture on the wall moves. It is a picture of clouds, high summer clouds. They look real enough to touch. I stand up and reach towards the picture. I can almost feel the cold cloud mist on my fingers after the hot glass of tea.

I am small again. My mother cradles me. I reach up, furious I cannot grasp the clouds overhead. My mother sings. It is a song about clouds. I watch them float past, one becoming the other, one becoming two. My mother's melody floats. Two becoming one. There is honey on her tongue. I am sleepy. I am sleeping in my mother's arms.

Nicolás clears his throat and I return at once to the table, and sit down again across from him.

"Perhaps you could repay me for the 'English lessons' with a favor. A very small favor," he says.

There is a brown paper bag on the table. Nicolás writes on a piece of paper and hands it to me. I do not know what is in the bag, maybe something illegal and they will put me in jail.

"Relax, Basim. These are just two fortune cookies for friends of your Uncle Habib. Do you know where Riverside Drive is?"

"Yes, Mr. Nicolás."

"Good boy. It won't be so far if you ride your bike."

"What bike, sir?"

"The one somebody left for you. I forget his name. You must have seen it on the way in."

"The red one with the sparkles and the skinny tires?"

"That must be the one. You must deliver this bag on your way home. There is no charge," Nicolás says. "And pay close attention. It is one of your American lessons, one not in the book."

I cannot wait to ride the bike, my bike. I finish my tea in one swallow, and take up the bag, the slip of paper, and the letters for Uncle Habib to sign. Nicolás bows to me and puts his hand on my head. I think maybe he is a holy man, but I do not know what kind.

I am a little bit afraid. There are many laws about traffic and right-of-way. I did not pay such close attention because I walk or ride the bus or the subway. I am very careful. I ride up to Union Square to find Broadway and stay on Broadway so I do not get lost. It is a long way, but once the cars and buses speed ahead of me, I have the road to myself for a minute and I go very fast. The wind makes noise like thunder in my ears. I feel so free.

"Watch out!" I holler. "Here comes the camel jockey!"

I love my bike. I love my Uncle Habib.

"I did not buy you the bicycle, Basim. You must..."

"Yes, I know," I told my Uncle. "I must ask Nicolás."

"Yes, you must. And he asked that you bring the lawyer papers back to him. The lawyer wants to bring us before the court so that you may become my son."

"I would like that, Uncle Habib."

"Go now. Bring my friend my greetings. Tell him The Bronx is not so far. He must come visit me soon."

I kiss my Uncle. He is a very good man. Then I go down to the basement to get my bike. Auntie has given me an old bedsheet to cover it. I did not want plaster and dust falling on it.

Café Kundalini is not yet open. Nicolás is in the kitchen making a special dish for a customer. It looks like a celery root with stripes. He slices it so thin and so fast and the knife is so big and gleaming sharp I am afraid he will cut himself.

"That's why I keep my hands in my pockets. It's safer that way," Nicolás says.

He takes his hands out of his pockets to show me he has not cut himself. I look over at the cutting board. The odd root is sliced as thin as an onion skin.

"You are a magician," I tell him, and laugh.

"I do not think it's magic, Basim, just science without an explanation, like how you learned to read and write American just by touching the book. So what did you learn the other night on your errand?"

"You sent me to bad men," I tell him.

"Your Uncle is my dearest friend, Basim. Would I throw his nephew to wolves? Why do you say they are bad men?"

"They answered the door in their underwear."

Nicolás laughs. He pushes the sliced root from the cutting board into a pot of hot oil. It sizzles and hisses.

"If I had a quarter for every New Yorker who answered the door in less than full attire, I'd be astoundingly wealthy, my boy. Better steel yourself."

This is not the sort of advice my teachers give me at school. Uncle Habib thinks his friend is wise. I am not so sure.

"They were sitting on the couch together, under the same blanket."

"Was it cold?" Nicolás asks. He cuts green onions and adds them to the pot.

"Cold and raining," I say.

Nicolás shrugs his shoulders and turns his palms up in my Uncle's imitation of him. He is forcing me to say it.

"They are faggots."

Nicolás puts a cover on the pot and takes off his apron. He walks with me to the front door. We stand and look down Avenue A to the park. He puts his hand on my shoulder. It is a sunny afternoon, cool, with high white clouds. There are many people in the park.

"What do you see, Basim?"

"I see America."

I smile. I think it is a clever answer the teacher will like.

"Who is America for?"

I imitate my Uncle's imitation of him with my palms and shoulders up.

"That is your assignment: an essay, *Who Is America For?* One full page, in American. There's a notepad and pen waiting for you on a bench in the park. Lock up your bike first, the one the bad men bought for you."

"What? Why? Why did *they* buy me a bike?"

"One of the men has known your Uncle since your Uncle's first week in America, when the man—his name is Six—was only a little older than you are, Basim. He wanted to do something nice for your Uncle. But there is never anything Uncle Habib wants, so he says to buy a bicycle for his nephew, a red one that sparkles."

"Then, technically, the bicycle is a payment to my Uncle."

"The little lawyer is always in his office."

"If you please, sir, go easy on me."

"If it was easy, Basim, you'd already be a millionaire. Time for the essay," Nicolás says.

I nod to him and set off toward Tompkins Square Park. He

is a tough teacher and he does not forget.

I puzzle over the bike from the men my friends say are bad men. Must I give it back? The men did not seem bad to me. They were friends. That cannot be wrong.

The paper and pen are on a bench. No one has stolen them. I chain my bike to the iron fence and sit across from it so I can keep an eye on it. I watch people in the park: young and old, tall and short, thin and fat, white and brown and black, people alone and people together. Are they all Americans? I do not know.

The words do not come. It is easier to watch the clouds. They look like they will get caught on the tall trees overhead, very old sycamore trees that seem to hold up the sky.

The afternoon is mild and sunny. I watch the people. Like the clouds, they come and go, one by one and in groups, some light, some dark. A young African woman carries her baby in a pouch in front of her. She sits down on a bench and feeds her child. I think of my mother. An old man hobbles past with his cane, reminding me of my Uncle Habib. Two men sit down on another bench. They hook their little fingers together, what Americans call *pinkies*. They are like the men who bought my bicycle for me. I see they are friends.

I think of myself and how, if my Uncle had not sent for me after my mother died and my father disappeared, I might be in the militia, shooting guns and killing people, maybe getting killed. My friends do not like anybody, only themselves. They call me "camel jockey" and "towel head." They do not like niggers and faggots and stupid bitches. Who is left? If they ran things, America would be like an empty sky. Maybe my friends do not know everything.

I write some words on the paper. It is still strange to me to understand American without thinking about it. I wonder if I have lost my old writing, my old *abajadīyah*, but it is still there. That makes me happy. Soon the page is full, but I do not like most of it. I cross words out. There is not much left. It will have to do.

Across the way, a pretty girl who has been eyeing me, approaches.

"You have beautiful eyes," she tells me. "So deep. Is that your bike?"

"Yes," I say. "My... my... Uncle Habib got it for me."

"May I ride it?" the girl asks.

"Yes," I tell her, and go to unlock it. "But don't go too fast."

"I won't."

She can barely reach the pedals and the bike wobbles. I am a little worried. She sets off down one of the paths and seems to do all right. I wait for her. Soon she comes from the opposite direction. She has gone round the entire park. The girl smiles at me and waves. I wish she would keep her hands on the handlebars. I wait for her to come round again.

I wait a long time, but the girl does not come back. I do not know her name. I go to look for her. I ask people in the park and on the street, but no one has seen her. It is getting late. I run back to Nicolás, to tell him what has happened. He is waiting for me with a tray of tea.

"Nicolás, my bike is gone. My red bike!"

"Easy, Basim. Didn't you lock it up?"

"Yes, I did. But a girl wanted to ride it. She smiled at me. I told her she could, but then she didn't come back. No one has seen her."

"Ah..." Nicolás says, drawing out his breath. "The lesson of your Uncle with the cash box, was that not a good one?"

"Yes, but... but... I forgot."

"That is OK, Basim. Everyone makes mistakes. I will get your red bike back."

"But I will be late for supper. Auntie will be cross with me."

"I can fix that, too, my boy. Let me have your phone."

I give Nicolás my phone. He touches it and hands it back. I can only guess what he has done, who he has called.

"Now, let us have tea. I want to hear your essay."

The tea is again rosehips with honey. I show Nicolás my page of writing with almost everything crossed out.

"I see you have filled up the page with American writing."

"Yes, but most of it is not good, just some of it."

"Well, then read me the best part."

I take a sip of tea and clear my throat. I am nervous. I am afraid he will laugh when I do not want to be funny.

"Who is America for? America is for people who have nowhere else to go."

Nicolás says nothing. He raises his glass of tea and I raise mine to him. We clink them together.

"That is good, Basim. If I were your teacher in school, I'd give you an 'A.' You will be a great American some day."

I smile and look out the window. It is almost dark. There is a rumbling outside. Two men ride up on a motorcycle. They take off their helmets and come inside. It is the two men I saw in their long underwear. They are wearing blue jeans and leather jackets. They look very cool. I feel very ashamed.

The men shake Nicolás's hand and laugh.

"I believe you know Basim, but he may not know your names."

I stand up and shake their hands. I feel very small next to them.

"Six will take you home, Basim. Antonio and I have business to discuss. Don't forget to leave your Uncle's papers here."

I wonder what kind of name "Six" is. He is blond with blue eyes. The other man is more like me: dark skin and eyes and hair.

Antonio hands me his helmet. I feel so cool. But it falls over my eyes. I make a joke.

"Maybe the towel-head needs a towel," I say.

Everyone laughs. Nicolás comes back from the kitchen with a towel and winds it around my head.

"Basim is studying to be an American," he says. "I guess he's now got another lesson down: Laugh at yourself before somebody beats you to it."

They laugh again. The helmet fits perfectly now. I see myself in the glass front door. Yes, I am pretty cool. I wish my friends could see me.

I sit at the back of the motorcycle. Six warns me the muffler is hot. I hold onto the belt of his leather jacket. Now I am worried my friends really might see me—see me with one of the men they call faggots. No, I don't care if they do see us. They will be jealous.

The engine is very loud and the motorcycle goes very fast.

At the red light I move forward and hold onto the pockets of Six's jacket. We take off like a rocket. It is scary and I do not want to look—but I do. I am flying like Prince Husain on his magic carpet.

We go onto the big highway in The Bronx. I have never gone so fast. I hide behind Six to escape the wind. I am cold. I watch the buildings race past me, and the road beneath me is a blur. I look up. I am flying as fast as the clouds.

There are not so many streetlights now. At last I see we are on City Island Road going through the park. Then we cross the old iron bridge and I am home.

I want to kiss the ground. My legs are sore. It was like riding a donkey, a donkey with the devil after him. I take off my helmet

"How'd you like it, Sport?" Six asks me.

"Fantastic," I tell him. I think it may be OK to tell a small lie to make someone feel good.

Uncle Habib and Auntie Moona come out to see what all the noise is about. They both hug Six. Then they hug me. They pull him inside and tell him he must stay for supper. He does not even try to turn them down.

We have goat stew with carrots and salad with lentils. I am glad there is enough for everybody. I am very hungry.

"It is a shame about the bicycle," my Uncle remarks, as though talking to no one.

I nod. I do not know how much Uncle Habib knows of the story. I hope he does not ask me anything. I cannot lie to Uncle Habib.

"Nicolás has said he will get it back for me, Uncle."

"And then you will owe him another favor."

"Yes, Uncle, I know."

"Antonio brought the bolt-cutters," Six tells my Uncle.

My Uncle shushes him. They smile at one another. I do not know what bolt-cutters are, but I will find out.

I see how my Auntie and my Uncle are with Six, how gentle they are. I see how they love one another. I see it in their eyes, in their smiles. My Uncle Habib would never love a bad man, nor would my Auntie.

Six gets up from the table. He kisses Auntie and thanks her

for the meal. Auntie says Uncle made the stew.

"There will be more visits from the social workers, Habib, but you have all been through that before. I think it wouldn't hurt to point out little Basim's new mastery of English."

I do not like Six calling me little. I am taller than Uncle Habib and almost as tall as him.

"When do you want me to swing by again, Sport, so you can pick up your bike?"

"He found it?" I ask.

"With Nicolás on the case, Basim, it's only a matter of time. Later, dude."

Six hugs Uncle and kisses Auntie and goes down the stairs. I hear him start up his motorcycle. I wave from the window.

I think I like Six. Maybe not as much as my Auntie and Uncle do, but he is OK for a faggot. Now that I know I will get my red bicycle back, I can think about the next thing to wish for. I think I would like a pair of blue jeans. I am going to be an American some day, a great American, as Nicolás says. I need to get ready.

———————◦———————

That night I have strange dreams. Those are the only kind I have. If things are not too strange, I know I must be awake.

It is not a magic carpet I am on, it is my bed that's flying. I roll to the edge and look down. I see all of New York, all the lights sparkling. I wonder why I am not terrified to be so high up. I see Uncle Habib's house and the park and the Statue of Liberty and my school, all of it as tiny as toys. Six and Antonio go by on a motorcycle in their long underwear.

Then I am standing with my Uncle and Auntie in the court. The Judge stands at the top of a ladder and looks down at us. I am a lawyer. I have papers. I address the Judge.

"Please, Sir Judge. There are enough laws in America. We need only one law."

"And what law is that, Basim?" the Judge asks.

I turn to my Uncle Habib. He smiles at me like the rising sun.

"Be kind," I tell the Judge. "Just be kind."

———————◦◦———————

Six comes by for me the next Friday. He brings two packages, a big square one and a flat one. It is my own helmet—one that fits me, a red one—and a pair of blue jeans. I go to my room to try them on while Uncle Habib and Six have a discussion over tea.

I hate the blue jeans. They are stiff and scratchy. Putting them on is like trying to get dressed in a cardboard box. I cannot sit or walk in them; everything rubs.

I want to wear the blue jeans Six has brought me, but I put my old tan trousers back on. They are so comfortable. Six sees I have not changed.

"Maybe your Auntie will wash the new jeans for you a couple times," he tells me. "They will get softer."

His jeans look soft, but these jeans are impossible. Americans must be crazy to wear blue jeans.

Uncle Habib and Six finish their discussion and their tea.

"Ready, Sport?"

I nod to Six and kiss my Uncle good-bye. Everything he wants to tell me is in his eyes. I am a little bit happy, a little bit scared. He touches my head in blessing

I ask Six if we can drive by my school, what my friends call the "Hairy Ass Truman High School." My friends will be sitting outside on the steps, passing judgment on the world.

We stop. There they are. They pretend they are looking somewhere else, but they are checking out the motorcycle. I unfasten the strap and take off my helmet. I wave to them.

My friend Bonkers waves back. The others nudge him. They pretend not to see me and how cool I am. Their mouths hang open like a bunch of stupid boys.

I put on my helmet and tap Six's shoulder. I hang on tight. He revs the engine and takes off so fast the front wheel rises in the air. He is showing off for my friends.

It is cold and I am glad I have on a sweater under my jacket. I think about many things on the drive to Nicolás's café in

Manhattan. I found out on the Internet what bolt-cutters are and I found out a faggot is a homosexual, a man who likes men. I do not really understand the fuss. I am more worried that Six's friend Antonio may have done something unlawful with the bolt-cutters and been sent to a prison.

Six finds a parking space near the front door of the café. We take off our helmets.

"Will you tell me what the bolt-cutters are for?" I ask Six.

He seems surprised. He stops.

"I don't want to go against your Uncle, Basim, but you seem a smart young man. How did you think we were going to get your bike back?"

I shrug and raise my hands. I had not thought about the how.

"Nicolás spotted your bike a couple streets over, chained to a street pole. It was your chain but not your lock. He stood guard while Antonio cut the chain on either side of the lock."

Six reaches into his jeans pocket and gives me the new lock and keys. They are warm in my cold hand.

"But you stole it from the poor girl."

"Yeah, from the girl who stole it from *you*. By the time we filed a report and made nice to the parents and wheedled the girl into giving the bike back, you'd have been too old to ride it. Nicolás said the bolt-cutters were a shortcut around the law. Come on. I need something warm."

I do not think I like the idea of shortcuts to the law, but I am happy to find my red bike in the kitchen. I look for scratches. Nicolás is making hot cocoa with cinnamon for us.

Six finds the table where Antonio is sitting and bends over to kiss him.

"You are homosexuals, right?" I ask them.

Six and Antonio sputter and look at each other. Then they laugh.

"I guess that's letting the cat out of the cellophane bag," Antonio says. "Yes, Basim. Most men like women, but some men like other men, like Six and me."

"That's like gay, right?"

"Six and me like *queer*, Basim. That's another word for odd or strange."

"So if my friends say you're faggots, I'll tell them you're queers."

"I'm not sure that will help much," Six says, smiling.

I think I understand, but American is such a queer language. Everything means something else—or three other things. How do Americans understand each other?

Nicolás brings four steaming mugs of cocoa. He sits down next to me and winks.

I feel like a man tonight. Six did not tell me a nice lie. He told me the truth. He is a good man. I know why my Uncle loves him. I love him, too. And Antonio.

———————◗○◖———————

It is the day for me and Auntie Moona and Uncle Habib to stand up in the court and speak with the Judge. I am nervous. I could not eat breakfast.

Today I am wearing the blue jeans from Six. They are the newest and darkest pants I have. They are still scratchy, but not so much. I think they help me stand straighter, but I do not like them. Maybe if I rub them in the dirt again, Auntie will give them another washing.

We stand looking up at the Judge. The lawyer, Mr. Juan de Crisco, does all the talking. Papers go back and forth, up and down. It is like my friends playing cards in the parking lot.

"Young man," the Judge says to me.

My face is burning. My tongue is stuck. I step forward.

"I was sorry to learn of the loss of your parents, my boy. But I was happy to hear that your Uncle and Auntie love you so much they want to adopt you."

I like that the Judge calls her Auntie, too. I think I like him.

"Your Uncle will be your Father from now on. You do understand the difference, don't you, young man?"

"Yes," I tell him. I am nervous; my voice shakes. "My Father will be stricter than my Uncle."

The Judge smiles. "Exactly so. And what, would you say, is the most important lesson your new Father has taught you?"

"To be kind," I say, as I did in my dream.

The room turns fuzzy and all the talking seems far away and mumbled. I grow dizzy. I wish I'd had breakfast. I faint, hitting my head on something. Then I see the polished stone floor.

I awaken on a wooden bench with my Auntie and Uncle, and the lawyer and even the Judge standing over me.

"Welcome to America, Basim," he says, and pats my arm. "Sit up slowly."

I learn from Mr. de Crisco that the adoption is approved. I am now my Uncle's son and the nephew of my Father. I am now an American, too. And I am wearing my blue jeans.

The lawyer shows me the papers with my name on them in American. My Auntie and Uncle hug and kiss me—I mean my new Mother and Father. I think I will begin wishing next for a motorcycle. I am not yet old enough to drive, but it will take time to find the one I like. It will have to be a red one.

I'M NOT WHO I WAS

I was having what they called a TLI, a Temporary Loss of Identity. They thought my implanted chip had malfunctioned. Since they didn't seem sure, I wondered whether the *temporary* could also have been mere speculation.

I sat in the common room of a windowless compound. There were five others, a woman and four men, whose identities had also gone missing. They all looked bewildered. In truth, there were windows, but the external steel shutters were always drawn down. I wondered whether our fugitive identities were congregating somewhere in cyberspace. I was the last to arrive here and, because I didn't remember my name, everyone, including the doctors and staff, called me Six. I doubted I was only the sixth person afflicted with Temporary Loss of Identity.

My compatriots also had conditional names and identities which they must return if their real selves ever turned up. None of us had laid eyes on each other before. Phineas had arrived six months ago, the others, less than that. I had been there for four days—what, without daylight, I judged to be days. We all shared the same implanted factual information—nearly everyone on the planet—but our personalities were our own. That was what was stored on our malfunctioning identity chips. Of course, some of who we are resides in our gray matter, too, but it was never clear to science what part of "I" was biologic and what part electronic. So I accepted my confusion and disorientation as the human condition.

On Thursday our keepers brought large sheets of drawing paper and pens, pencils, and crayons. I speculated that they wanted to see what natural talents we possessed, a combination of innate proclivities and muscle memory. It was an intriguing idea, the answer to which might have given a small clue to our identities. I figured our aptitude with musical instruments and electronic circuit boards would be tested next.

I used the pencils and crayons to render an accurate depiction of our common room and everyone in it. It was the only image I had to draw upon. The rest of my memory vanished along with "me." Mine was the only drawing that bore any resemblance to our surroundings. The other inmates drew colored boxes and stick figures.

Dr. Mallow stepped away from the long table, holding her hands behind her back and making indecipherable faces. She stood behind me and placed a hand on my shoulder. When I looked up from my drawing, I saw the room was empty. The others must have been dismissed.

"You have obviously rendered depictions by hand before, Six," she said. "Were you perhaps an artist?"

Her question was undoubtedly intended to nudge something loose. I shrugged.

"What else can you draw?"

"What else is there?" I asked. "Just my cell."

"We prefer the word cubicle. It has friendlier connotations."

Her horseshit was getting deep. I said nothing, but I saw my scowl in the shutter-darkened window glass. I wondered whether my nature had always been so combative.

Dr. Mallow pressed her thumb on an ID screen beside the steel shutters. The far-right one rolled up, creaking and grating. The sunlight hurt my eyes. I squinted until the rough shapes acquired detail.

In the middle-ground I saw a procession of wooden poles across the landscape. Their crossbars and wires had long ago fallen down. Beyond that were steep hills covered with scrubby brush and scarred with gulches and gullies. In the distance, beneath a brilliant blue sky and fair cumulus clouds, was an encircling arc of tall, snow-covered peaks, some rounded, some jagged. The vegetation, which I took to be sagebrush, marched right up to the window. On the hills and mountains stood pine trees and deciduous trees in the process of turning to gold in the sunlight.

"Thank you," I told the doctor. Unconsciously, my left hand raced across the drawing tablet bearing a blue crayon. My right hand held other colors. I realized I was most interested in the sky.

"Aren't you curious about where you are?"

"It wouldn't change the scenery by giving it a name," I remarked.

"No? Are you sure?" She tilted her head like Nipper, the RCA mascot. "We're in The Aspens. Mean anything to you?"

I shook my head, shutting my eyes for a second to scan the *Omnia Omnium, The All of Everything* for the reference. I continued drawing. The crayon snapped when I realized what sort of clouds I'd been drawing: mushroom clouds.

"This is where the first nuclear device was detonated," I told her.

"Precisely," Dr. Mallow replied. "We remain a research facility to this day."

The shutter rolled down. I realized I was sad to be closed away from the world again. I noticed a tear streak down Six's face, my face, in the dark, reflective glass.

Thereafter, Dr. Mallow allowed me two hours per awake cycle in the common room with my watercolors and the hand-pressed papers she brought me from Santa Fe. She did not ask Six for money. I don't know whether I had any, either. She did not pester me to see any of the sketches. She could have flipped through the stack of drawings whenever she wanted anyhow.

I felt the most comfortable with the watercolors , the most connected to my brushes and paints—and the water itself. The images flowed from me, from my fingers, and spread through the fibers of the rough paper. It seemed I could draw nothing but clouds. That hardly mattered to Six Thorson, whom I decided deserved a last name. It was my name, too, I figured. I'd no idea from where it popped into my head. Maybe it was my real name bubbling up.

Though we were told our cells were locked at night, mine

was not. I'm not sure what prompted my trying the handle. The door swung open. No lights or sirens went off. I walked to the common room in my bathrobe and shower sandals, and stared with dismay at the closed shutters. Six put my thumb on the ID panel. We concentrated on sending it the mental signal to roll up, though I myself knew telekinesis was hogwash.

The metal shutters were heavy, containing, as I learned, lead shielding. They groaned and squeaked. The effort wore me out and Six got a banging headache. But the shutters, all four of them, were more than half-raised. A nearly full moon hung over the distant mountain range, illuminating the snow caps. I could not tell at first whether the moon was rising or setting, but the gradually diminishing shadows of the sagebrush suggested it was rising. It also told me the arc of mountains lay to the east.

I sat in the common room contentedly enjoying the moon-lit scenery. When the moon had risen beyond the upper edge of the windows, I decided to return to my cell. Trying with all my might, I could not lower the steel shutters. Six was already asleep. I figured our keepers would simply think the shutters had mal-functioned. They seemed to like malfunction as an explanation, though it explained nothing. I fell asleep trying to understand how Six had raised the shutters without touching anything.

The next morning, after the customary breakfast of fruit, cheese, bread, and coffee, Dr. Mallow took me to the common room. None of my identity-challenged compatriots was present. The other three staff doctors stood there in their white lab coats holding clipboards.

"Six, how did you raise the security shutters last night?" Dr. Mallow asked. "It was a rather serious breach."

She introduced me to Dr. Egad De Bockel, a Dutch/Israe-li neuroscientist with a special interest in recovery from serious brain injury. He shook my hand weakly. Six thought of a dead flounder. I told him to pipe down.

"I beg your pardon," Dr. De Bockel said.

"That's all right, Doctor. You are forgiven," I replied. "We are all forgiven."

I had no idea from which cerebral fold that idea emanated, but it did not seem to concern the doctors. Perhaps forgiveness meant nothing to them. Dr. De Bockel continued with his questioning.

"We'd like to measure your brain activity, Six, while you raise the shutters again. With your permission, of course."

"I haven't a clue how I did it, Doctor. If I don't agree, you'll force me anyway, right?"

The four doctors looked back and forth and across at one another as though taking in a slow tennis match. The chair and its wired helmet bore a resemblance to a 1950s hair drying hood in a women's beauty salon.

"Will my hair get curly?" Six asked.

This time the doctors seemed amused and their body language suggested they were more relaxed. I lowered myself into the chair and they strapped me in. The helmet was heavy. They put goggles over my eyes and asked if I were comfortable. Six was against my cooperating with them in this way, afraid they might probe for more than they admitted they were seeking.

Of course, I knew Six and I were the same person—and there were more of us in here. Or were they out there? Were they the other inmates here whose memories and identities were also lost? Or was I imagining them all? I didn't know. I worked on that puzzle when I should have been trying futilely to raise the shutters by the power of thought alone.

Dr. Mallow recommended removing my goggles, suggesting that visual feedback might be a necessary component of telekinesis. The other doctors didn't laugh, so I assumed they bought into her hooey. I wondered whether they knew there was no such thing as a self, either.

I felt less claustrophobic without the goggles and leaned back. I loved challenges, too. Nicolás, one of my other persons inside, suggested I might want to give my keepers a small demonstration just to remain on their good sides. It might procure me continued preferential treatment. Basim, a thoroughly logical and judicious fellow, also thought I should give them a little token until we had time to consider other options. Antonio and Hypatia opposed all cooperation—with any authority. They were quite adamant. It was up to me to break our tie.

Squinting and grunting, I turned slightly to one side and pictured the shutters going up. I heard and saw nothing budge. Then there was light-hearted chatter and laughter among the doctors standing behind me. They asked me to turn around.

The four doctors' lab coats had been turned inside out and pulled up to their necks like funnels. They looked like unfortunate pets inside their plastic cones. I laughed, as did everyone else in my head. The doctors were less amused. Antonio thought I should leave them like that and go back to our cell. I was inclined to put it to a vote, but thought, *What the hell? Who's the boss around here anyway?*

As I thought about it, the helmet, arm straps, and sensors lifted off of me. I walked to the doorway and touched my thumb to the entry ID panel and thought the door open—politely, as Nicolás urged. *It works better than being unpleasant.* I turned to the four doctors, struggling inside their inverted lab coats.

"Apparently, visual cues are indeed an important element of telekinesis," I told them, though I did not believe a word of it.

The door slid shut behind me, and I returned to our cell.

———◦———

I was brought to the common room the next morning by two attendants in white, one at each elbow.

Dr. Juan de Crisco, the eminent Spanish psychiatrist, scowled at me and told me my little demonstration the day before had exhibited "extreme hostility to authority."

"You betcha," Hypatia said, but, fortunately, she did not have the floor in my head, and nothing came out of my mouth but a silent grin.

"You think this is funny?" the fourth doctor asked. "I assure you we are deadly serious. I am not opposed to dissection— or vivisection, for that matter."

General Warren Pease, surgeon general under two administrations, was no doubt likeable in a family situation. But I was not a member of his family, nor did I wish to be.

"For the record," he went on, glancing up at one of the security cameras, "I opposed this experiment. What good can be derived from allowing even one individual to exist beyond the reach of surveillance?"

"This, General Pease," Dr. Mallow said, gesturing, "is the first fully documented instance of telekinesis. Tell me you do not imagine military applications for such abilities."

"Yeah, but how do you control somebody like him? He's a loose cannon, a freak of nature."

"Just for the record," I interrupted. "I don't believe in telekinesis."

"That's rich," Dr. de Crisco said. "So what raised the shutters last night?"

"Um... an anti-gravity ray?" I offered. "Ask the General. That's his department."

They angrily slammed down their clipboards, except for Dr. Mallow. I expected them next to rend their lab coats. Instead they went to the sliding entrance door to the common room and took turns showing it their thumbs. Hypatia and Antonio decided it would be fun to frustrate them and held the doors for a while. The doctors looked to Dr. Mallow for help.

"Say *Please*," I instructed them.

General Pease let out an insincere one-syllable laugh. When, finally, Dr. De Bockel said the magic word, Antonio and Hypatia released the doors. But then they would not let them close.

"Don't forget the *Thank you*," I recommended.

After some minutes passed, the General, growling, uttered the magic incantation. Before the doors closed, I reminded them that no one was too big or important to be polite.

"You are not making friends here, Six," Dr. Mallow told me.

I wanted to tell her I wasn't the one who had held the doors, but I wondered how much she understood of the unfettered mind—or even of the fettered kind.

It should have occurred to me I'd be under constant sur-veillance in a secret government facility. I don't know what I could've done differently. I had no idea I could move things with my mind and had no idea how I did it, making it, in my opinion, useless for any practical effect. It could not be relied on.

I became aware of sitting in the common room facing the four raised shutters and looking at the night sky. I had no recollec-tion of leaving my cell or raising the steel shutters. I stood trans-fixed by the mystically beautiful landscape

The moon was somewhere behind the facility. The sage-brush sparkled, as though from a recent rain, though there were no clouds I could see. The four illuminated rectangles from the windows trailed out into the night and melted in the shadows. I shut my eyes. Six longed to breathe in the aroma of the rain-fresh-ened air and the sweet, smoky, camphory smell of the sagebrush. Was that another of my memories bubbling up?

Feeling a stir of air, I figured the party was over. I hoped it was Dr. Mallow who had entered. Opening my eyes, I was shocked to see I was no longer inside The Aspens facility.

I stood outside on the damp ground completely naked. The chilly breeze gave me a shiver. I shut my eyes and filled my lungs with the desert air, air washed by rain and lightning and suffused with the masculine aroma—like antiseptic or gin—of the sagebrush. I'd become slightly aroused. The moon peered from behind an intricate mantilla of clouds.

Once Six breathed our fill, it was time to figure out how we were all going to get back inside the facility. I thought it might be important to face in the direction in which I wanted to transport myself. After turning around, I looked through the windows of the dimly-lit common room, so sterile and unimaginative after beholding the rain-drenched desert by moonlight.

I closed my eyes again and thought of the heated common room. It had no particular smell, not even of plastic. When the sagebrush aroma faded, I knew I was back inside the facility. My robe and sandals lay beneath the third window. I put them on, wondering how this would look on their security cameras. Hypatia, the only woman inside me, laughed wickedly.

The doctors pestered me about these "nocturnal egressions." It was easy to claim ignorance. I truly did not know how any of this happened since it was clearly impossible. At last they convinced themselves that my teleportation was akin to somnambulism and that I would be expected to remember none of it.

Through trial-and-error I discovered several rules about my getting on the other side of things. I didn't want to let the doctors know what I was up to, so I projected myself outdoors directly from my cell. I made a dummy of blankets and sheets and pillows to disguise my absence. Going further into the desert, I escaped their cameras and motion and infrared sensors.

Teleportation did indeed require one to face in the direction of travel. You could bring objects with you, but you had to be in contact with them and remain aware of them throughout. I once brought my drawing pad with me, but it lodged halfway out of the wall when I forgot it for a second. I used my other impossible ability, telekinesis, to extract the sketch pad.

It was easiest to wear longjohns, a sweatshirt, and thick socks. They usually made the trip outside with me. For some reason I continually became unaware of one or the other of my shoes, and it fell wherever it was that I'd stopped concentrating on it.

Often I came back wearing less on purpose. Beneath a cluster of pine trees, I'd squirreled away a nylon bag, and filled it with extra clothing, purloined from the lockers of the maintenance workers. My pencils and hand-drawn maps made it outside on later excursions. My notebook and sketchbook would escape with me on the last night.

Antonio could not sleep for his excitement at "springing this joint." Six and the teacher Nicolás were in his camp. Basim imagined only dire consequences—eating garbage or starving—for a vagrant without an identity chip. Phineas looked forward to an adventure, but he was quite aware things do not often go as intended. He dared Antonio to project himself outside in daylight, a gauntlet Antonio readily took up.

Yes, they were all me, and all of us were going to escape—as soon as we could work out the details.

———◦———

Dr. Mallow detected my nervousness. It was the day Antonio planned to project himself outside in broad daylight. I'd be with Dr. Mallow and perhaps one or more of her colleagues. It meant adding another impossible ability, bilocation, to my resume. I did not believe in any of this, but I had faith Antonio and I could pull it off. He would be the distraction we needed in order for all of us to escape.

"Where are the others?" I asked the doctor.

"What others, Six? Do you mean my colleagues?"

I saw her puzzlement. I shrugged and smiled, realizing my fellow captives at the facility had, without doubt, been residing solely in my head all along.

"Just thinking of someone I knew," I said. "Her name's Hypatia."

"A memory?" the doctor postulated.

"In another lifetime, perhaps," I replied to her.

"Fourth-century Alexandria?" she asked. "Do you time-travel, too?"

I shook my head. Traveling through time was even impossibler than my other supposed talents. Phineas, I knew, had been a railroad foreman before the Civil War. Hypatia lived a long time before that, before any of us. Basim was an Iranian refugee who became a New York State Supreme Court Judge. Nicolás was a teacher in pre-Communist Cuba. Antonio was a gay biker from New Mexico. We were pretty mixed company.

I turned so that Dr. Mallow would look past me and out the window at Antonio. Her expression registered her shock. I turned away from the Doctor and closed my eyes, picturing myself standing in the space occupied by Antonio. I let my government-issued jumpsuit fall to the floor before projecting myself outdoors.

Hypatia howled with delight at being free—and naked. She and Antonio danced around a scraggly piñon as though it were a maypole. Phineas and Basim consulted the maps and laid out our route. I reached my bag of stashed clothing and got dressed.

I would have liked to see what sort of notes Dr. Mallow wrote up about the incident, but none of us had any intention of returning to the lab merely to have a chuckle at her expense. Our freedom had its cost, but it was one we bore gladly. Besides, I liked Dr. Mallow. She had been the friendliest person at the laboratory.

No one at The Aspens heard from any of us again, though, no doubt, they are still peering beneath every clump of sagebrush and sweeping the shadows, looking for traces of those who might never have existed except in my head.

I stand at the edge of the highway in dusty Levi's, jean jacket, and cowboy boots that look as though they'd walked across the entire Southwest diagonally. There's a bedroll slung over my right shoulder. I've no idea where I am going or where I've been. It doesn't matter.

I cross the highway to the Sagebrush Diner, no traffic in either direction as far as eye can see. The two cars and three trucks bear New Mexico license tags. The newest vehicle is from the late 1940s. I am famished.

The five men at the counter are dressed similarly in dusty boots and blue jeans. I leave an empty seat and sit down on the next red leatherette stool.

"What'll it be, Six?" the red-headed waitress asks. She looks down over her glasses at me.

I wonder for a minute how she knows me. Is it because I am the sixth man at the counter? In the diamond-pattern quilted stainless steel wall behind her, I see my distorted reflection. On my faded blue T-shirt is a backward white number six.

"The usual, Fanny," I say, taking a chance I know her, too. Her name is sewn onto her white blouse.

"You got 'er."

Each of the other five men at the counter nods at me in the quilted wall.

"Mornin', Six," recites the male chorus.

I'm pleased to note I am not disliked in these parts. Fanny whisks past, leaving a welcome cup of black coffee. She has the handle turned towards my left hand. I pick it up and inhale the steam before swallowing. It clears my head. I feel as though I've awakened after sleeping for twenty years.

GRANDMA'S SOUP

The winter after my tenth birthday, my parents went off on a "second honeymoon" to Mexico. They were driving my Dad's brand new tan-and-burgundy Hudson with whitewalls the size of Saturn's rings. I had no notion what honeymoons entailed. Nine months to the minute later, my sister came home from the hospital, but I never put the two events together.

My grandmother, my father's mother, lived with us in our one-bedroom *casita*. She got the bedroom. My parents slept in the dining room where my own small bed and chest of drawers occupied an antipodal corner. Sheets did double-duty as tablecloths. There was talk of Uncle Nicolás building a dividing wall if the landlady permitted it. Mom had already picked out the wallpaper, and taped samples to the rough stucco of the existing walls.

It was two weeks after Thanksgiving and it was colder than anyone in northern New Mexico recalled. Everything freezable froze, from pumps to automobile engines. A farmer up the road claimed his wood-fire froze and wouldn't give no more heat. Mom and Dad got away in the nick of time.

Thankfully, our pump was indoors in the kitchen not three feet from the stove. My friend at school, Antonio, had to bring in snow to melt beside the hearth: one bucketful of snow to the teaspoon of water.

Grandma promised me her homemade soup. We'd eat it for the rest of the week, but I didn't mind. She knew it was my favorite. I agreed to haul in more firewood.

It was so cold my eyeballs steamed up once I came back inside. I saw three Grandmas gathered around the stove like Macbeth's witches stooped over their cauldron.

"Double bubble," she said.

I smiled at her joke. Setting my armload of wood beside the stove, I noticed two loaves of bread rising in pans on the metal shelf above. If my Grandma loved me—and I knew she did—the bread would be laced with jalapeños and old, sharp cheddar from her friend with the goats.

"Do you wonder, Six, how I knew what you were thinking, about the witches?"

I shrugged. I hadn't considered it. She pulled her hand-knit shawl tighter and gave her long gray braids, tied with the same red and yellow and turquoise yarn, a slow, deliberate shake.

"It's not that I'm such a great listener, child, it's that you're a phenomenal talker, loud 'n' clear, better 'n your Great-Grandma, my Mama, even. You think it's your secret, but your *abuela* knows all about these things."

My face grew warm, standing too close to the stove, no doubt.

"Here, Six, you can help me cut things up for the soup."

Grandma set six big carrots, as many stalks of celery, and four potatoes on the cutting block beside the sink. She handed me a sharp knife, looking down over her glasses at me but not saying a word.

"I won't," I said, reading her thoughts. "I'll be careful." I set to work on the carrots, the next into the pot.

"You're listening to me, child, the same as if I was talking out loud, but I ain't. It's your gift. The celery's next. Then peel the potatoes, but I'll cut them."

"Yes, Grandma. Where did I learn to talk and listen without words?"

She pulled two big beef bones from the pot and set them on the drainboard to cool.

"Your gift comes from my Mama, your Great-Grandma. Didn't come to me, didn't come down to your Uncle Nicolás or your Daddy, either, though we can all do some things. Can you cut up a couple onions? They're next."

"Sure, Grandma. How big a pieces you want?"

"You ate my soup before. Pieces as big as those were. Your Great-Grandma passed the gift on to you on your birthday. Do you remember feeling it?"

"Nope. About this big?"

"Yes, child. A true boy you are. You pay no attention to what's going on inside. You'll have to learn to listen to yourself if you're going to help anybody else."

The bones now cool enough, she pulled the meat off with her fingers and ripped it into small pieces she dropped back in the soup along with the bones. I finished peeling the potatoes and Grandma cut them up with a butcher's knife they were so hard. I liked hearing the pieces plop into the swirling water. I added the onions I'd cut up. My eyes burned and watered.

It was near sundown and I saw The Mountain outlined in rose and gold, with black and silver streaks reaching closer like a giant's fingers. The ferns of frost, fed by the vapors and aromas from the roiling pot of soup, grew across the window panes. Soon they would meet in the middle and cover the last of the sun. I shivered despite standing near the stove.

My Grandma and I continued our conversation both aloud and silently, like the bizarre table talk in our bilingual family that shifted from English to Spanish on the turn of a peso. She taught me a trick for skinning the tomatoes, cutting an X on the bottom and dropping them into boiling water for not even a minute. The skin nearly fell off.

After adding all the ingredients to the soup except for the shell-shaped macaronis that went last, Grandma took off her apron and we sat at the kitchen table. She took a bottle of Dos Equis from our rattletrap refrigerator and two glasses from the china cabinet in the corner. It was not my first taste of beer, but I pretended it was.

"You're not very good at keeping secrets, Six, except from yourself. And you're a bad actor. Well, at least you don't lie to yourself."

We jumped as the cap popped off the bottle of beer on its

own. Grandma looked at me with a scowl.

"Must've been bringing the cold beer into the warm room that did it," I told her.

"So why doesn't it happen in summer?" she shot back. Then she smiled, poured an equal amount of beer in each glass, and clinked mine with hers.

The beer grew warm before either glass was emptied. Grandma uncovered the rising loaves of bread and slipped them into the oven. I was hungry enough to eat one loaf by myself. She motioned me over to the stove.

"Now comes the most important part, Six: the spices. Without spice, everything, even life, is oatmeal. Pay attention. If anything happens to me, I don't know how much of this your Great-uncle Nicolás remembers. Your Father knows none of it, claimed it was a load of you-know-what. That's why most of the gifts bypassed him."

I did my best to pay attention but the beer and the hot kitchen made me sleepy. Salt, cracked peppercorns, laurel leaves, garlic, and rosemary from her garden were all seasonings with which I was familiar. A dash was smaller than a pinch but just as inexact.

She put her apron back on and stood on the stool from beneath the sink in order to reach the top shelf of her spice rack. She took down an array of oddly-shaped glass jars and tin boxes to reach a covered woven basket that looked a hundred years old. On a cloth tag written in ink was *A. muscaria*. After removing two pieces of dried mushroom, she took a third smaller piece from the bottom and dropped them into the soup. She returned everything to the topmost shelf.

"That's the most important spice in my soup, my boy, and the reason you must like it. *Mosca agaric* is also used as a poison, but if you slice the mushrooms and dry them on a red string, the poisons weaken and only the magic remains."

"Did you ever try drying it on a green string, Grandma?"

"No, I did not. That's not how I was taught."

"Maybe the color of the string has nothing to do with it."

"Go bring the butter in from the larder so it can get soft. I don't want to hear nonsense."

I put the crock of butter on the table and set our places. After filling a pitcher with water from the pump. Grandma added a couple splashes of anise extract and a measuring cup of sugar. I stirred it in silence. She wondered whether I was not listening or pouting, but I kept quiet.

Sampling the soup with her big wooden spoon, Grandma dumped in the shell-shaped macaronis and announced it would be finished soon. I couldn't wait.

I brought the bowls one by one over to the stove, holding them with a towel. She filled them with a huge blue-enameled ladle. After covering the pot and setting it to one side, she dumped the loaves from their pans, from which they were practically bursting, and cut four thick slices. As always, she claimed the heel.

Though the aromas made me ravenous, I slowed down to my Grandma's pace and slurped the soup with relish. Each ingredient remained distinct. The broth contained all the flavors, and the spices tickled my tongue one after the other. I slathered my bread with butter.

At the bottom of my bowl were all three mushrooms, now puffed up, their color restored: red with white spots.

"No, Six, it wasn't a mistake. You'll make better use of the mushrooms than I will."

I grew so sleepy I could barely stay upright in my chair. I begged to be able to do dishes in the morning. Grandma relented, and kissed me good night. Her hair smelled like the sagebrush smudge sticks she burned in her room.

I lit my Great-grandpa's old railroad lantern atop my dresser, drawing comfort from its warm glow. I felt strange, as though not all of me was in my body. The sheets were freezing even through my longjohns and flannel shirt. At last I stopped shivering and drifted off to sleep.

A noise startled me. I could not tell whether I were awake or dreaming. Every flicker of the lantern flame sent strange creatures scurrying across the walls and ceiling, chasing their tails in playful romps. Everything seemed alive, every crack in the wall a coursing river or a throbbing vein. I stood at the foot of my bed though I didn't recall crawling out from under the warm quilt and blanket.

The walls of my room grew thin, translucent, revealing the full moon and the reaching shadows of the aspen trees on the glistening snow outside. I was sure I was not dreaming. I felt cold air brush against my face and tousle my hair. My feet turned ice cold. Little by little, the walls and ceiling dissolved completely. I found myself standing in the back yard, barefoot in the snow, looking up at the moon and its halo of thin, icy rainbows. A chorus of coyotes echoed in the crystal air. I answered them.

At last the frozen snow registered pain on my naked feet. I stepped across the yard to the back door. It felt like walking on sharp gravel. The door was locked.

I didn't think I'd make it around the house to the front door, which was likely also locked, Grandma's custom whenever my father was not at home. I stepped to the other end of the yard, my feet now numb. I rapped hard on Grandma's window.

The shade flapped up, making a noise like startled crows in the barn loft. Grandma tugged at the sash and the window flew up.

"What are you doing out there, child? Get in here."

I boosted myself up to the sill and crawled through the window, tumbling onto the floor. Grandma helped me to my feet.

"The door was locked," I explained.

"Then how'd you get outside?"

"I don't know, Grandma."

"Let's get you into bed."

She brought an extra quilt from her room and folded it double over my legs. I still shivered and the numbness in my feet turned to prickling pain. I was getting warm and comfortable when she returned to my room and raised the quilt over my feet. She'd brought two adobe bricks heated on the stove and wrapped in newspaper, and placed them between my feet.

She replaced the quilt and came to kiss me good night, calling me her *amado nieto*—her beloved grandson. She did not speak Spanish very often, so I knew it was special.

"We'll talk more of your adventure in the morning, my child. You have greater gifts than anyone in our family that I know of. Maybe it's time to have a talk with your Uncle Nicolás."

Grandma turned down the old railroad lantern and left my room. I fell right to sleep.

When my sister Emma entered our family, I moved to Uncle Nicolás's house so she could have my old room. I wanted to stay with my Uncle, to live in his house, so I was careful to obey him. I loved Uncle Nicolás very much. But at fifteen I got a girl at school pregnant while I lived in his house.

It was a day in early autumn. The girl's name was Hypatia. I liked her. She was pretty, with fair skin, blonde hair, and hazel eyes, more like me than most of our classmates. She knew I liked boys more than girls, but she never tired of trying to turn me around. Every boy in school wanted to get under her skirt, but not me. I wasn't sure about my buddy Antonio.

"Do you think you'll ever make it with a girl?" Hypatia had asked me on the walk home from school after the bus dropped us off. "Otherwise you'll never have kids."

"There's always adoption," I replied.

We stopped at my gate, my Uncle Nicolás's house. Hypatia lived further up the road.

"Do you want to practice on me? I don't mind," she announced.

"We're too young to have a family, Hypatia. Neither of us even has an after-school job."

"We'll be careful. Don't you have any galoshes?"

"You mean rubbers. No, I don't."

"Well, I bet you can't even get stiff enough to put one on."

"Can so."

"Prove it."

My seduction now complete, I took Hypatia's hand and led her upstairs to my room. Hypatia lay back on my bed and made herself at home. I stood facing her at the foot of the bed. I did not expect my Uncle Nicolás for another couple of hours.

I'd been practicing hands-free sex, but only on myself. I

never even showed Antonio, afraid I'd scare him off. I didn't care if I scared Hypatia away. I hoped I did.

After kicking off my gym shoes, I dropped my sweatshirt and Levi's on the floor at the foot of the bed. Then I dropped my shorts and smiled at her, but Hypatia wasn't looking at my face.

My abilities had rules, I was learning, but I figured we were safe so long as I didn't touch her. I extended my arms over her but remained three feet away. She wore her cheerleader's outfit of orange and black, the school colors. I made hand and arm movements as though I had grabbed her sweater and pulled it over her head and off her arms. Off came her sweater, slowly, teasingly. As I suspected, she was not wearing a bra. I fondled her emerging breasts and tickled her nipples. She giggled.

"How do you do that?" Hypatia asked.

"Magic, I guess."

I tugged at her ugly pleated skirt without using my hands. She held onto the waistband, but released it little by little. Then I took off her ten-pound saddle shoes and drew off her underpants and socks.

"Six," she cooed, drawing my name out as though it contained a half-dozen vowels.

I got into the spirit of proving to Hypatia I could make love to her if I wanted, continuing my exploration of her hips and thighs and slender calves. I tickled the little bush between her legs, and then tickled her feet. Hypatia writhed and wriggled and made warbling noises. As I grew more excited watching her respond so enthusiastically to my "touch," my little friend stood up, encouraging me to go further.

When I thought she couldn't take any more teasing, I thrust my hips forward and pictured touching the tip of my penis to the lips of her vagina.

"Ooh, Six."

Each time I pushed forward, I imagined entering her a little deeper. Hypatia responded as though I were bent over her on the bed actually making love to her. I visualized going as far as I could into her. She moaned and panted and moaned again.

"Stop, Six. I can't take any more. I believe you. Yes, you are a real man. I'm sorry I made fun of you. Please, stop."

I did not need to prove anything. I'd learned that journeying to the edge held far more pleasure than jumping off of it. My arousal diminished, I slipped into my jeans and sweatshirt, and tied my sneakers.

Hypatia scooted to the edge of my bed and put on her clothes, looking often in my direction and grinning at me. Despite her big talk about being experienced with boys, I saw she had left a spot of blood on my quilt, one that was forever after a part of the design.

I walked Hypatia the rest of the way to her house and offered to carry her book bag.

"What's in here?" I asked. "Paving stones?"

"Mr. Archuleta, my math teacher, brought me some more books from the University library. I'm going to be a famous astronomer, you know."

"No, I didn't know, but if you say you are, I expect you will, Hypatia."

"Thank you, Six, for believing in me."

"Thanks for our little practice session back at the house," I told her.

When we reached her gate I handed over her book bag, and kissed her on the cheek.

———◦———

"But, Uncle Nicolás, I had Grandma's soup in my Thermos for lunch that day and Hypatia still got pregnant. How could this happen?"

"Your Grandma's soup is not a prevention to anything, you know," my Uncle said, shaking his head. "You must have done something, Six."

"I do not know how she became *embarazada*. I did not lay a finger on her. I do not like girls in that way."

He set the gnarled fork of an old cottonwood on the block, a log that would resist a maul and wedge, and maybe even dynamite. It required as much effort whether I used my brain or my muscles to split the wood, and I sweat just the same. I shut my eyes and quartered it. Uncle Nicolás picked up the pieces and tossed them onto the growing mound of firewood.

"You do not believe me, Uncle. Now I know how Saint Joseph must have felt."

"That was different. The Holy Ghost was involved in that one. I know you are an honest boy, Six. You are a good boy. But you do not know your gifts, your power. You may die without knowing all you can do."

Uncle Nicolás set another log on the block and waited for me to split it. I divided it in four again without using the axe. He threw the pieces onto the pile.

"I know you are angry, but, please, make bigger pieces, not kindling," he said. "Come. I am tired. Let's have a beer."

Uncle's beer was not very cold. While he'd had electricity brought to the house, he complained the refrigerator made too much noise and kept him awake, so it was not plugged in. He opened the refrigerator door at night when it was cool and closed it first thing in the morning.

After snapping off the caps, he handed me a bottle and we sat on the wooden bench on the shady side of the house.

"Have you and Hypatia thought of names for the boy?"

"It might be a girl."

"No, it won't, Six," he replied, taking a swallow of beer.

"How come you know so much more than Grandma, Tio Nicolás?"

I made my beer cold. Sweat dripped from the bottle. My Uncle took another gulp of his warm beer.

"Your Grandma thinks she will never forget anything, which is why she doesn't remember hardly anything. I recall what your Great-grandma, *tu bisabuela*, said would come to pass because I wrote it down. I still have my notebook. I will live many years yet. It is your son, Six, who will close my eyes."

I held my cold bottle to my forehead. Behind Uncle's back I continued to chop wood.

"Why are you still sweating, Six? Are you still chopping wood?"

I could not lie to him and admitted I was. I wanted to have a free day tomorrow so I could go hiking with Antonio. Uncle looked at me sternly and then cracked a smile.

"You are stubborn, like a burro, like my Papa for whom you were named: Sixtus van Thorson. You must not be so pig-headed, so *testarudo*, Six. Come. That's enough work for one day. Let's have another beer."

Uncle returned with two bottles and an old photo of my *bisabuelo*, my great-grandfather, he'd shown me a dozen times. Again I chilled only mine because Uncle didn't like his beer cold.

"You even have his eyes and hair color, Six," he said, showing me the picture. It was an old sepia photo and he looked Spanish to me, but I did not contradict my Uncle.

"Will Hypatia and I get married?" I asked him.

"No, Six. My Mama said you would not ever get married."

"Will I always be alone?"

"No, you will have a best friend for your whole life."

"Antonio?" I asked.

"I don't remember. I will have to look it up. But I do remember *tu bisabuela* said you would always be happy, and kind to everyone."

Uncle tapped the lip of his bottle against mine and winked.

"To the future," he said. "To your future."

That night, though I hadn't meant to, I stacked all the firewood in my sleep. Uncle said it dried best when piled up in the shape of a teepee. When Antonio came to fetch me at dawn for our hike down into The Gorge, I did not awaken until he came to my room and shook me.

———◦———

Hypatia came over to Antonio's house, the *casita* he inherited from his grandparents, with little José. I knew Uncle Nicolás had wanted us to name him Jesús because of how Hypatia got pregnant. He liked to make fun of the Church, but Hypatia and I decided on José.

Hypatia unloaded a carload of José's things. It looked like

we would have to add a room to the house just for the boy's toys.

"I'm sorry, Six," she said. "I wanted to spend some time before dashing off, but I forgot about the stupid time change, like cutting an end off a blanket and sewing it onto the other end to make it longer. I don't want to keep my ride to Santa Fe waiting. Where's Antonio?"

José wriggled from her grasp and toddled over to stand on my foot and hug my thigh.

"Antonio's working. Big job coming up, lots of stonework and mature trees. We'll have to get Hermione to watch José on the days we're both working."

I heard a crash upstairs, but the boy continued to amuse himself running in and out between me and his mother.

"I swear there's two of him sometimes," Hypatia said. "I'll be back at Christmas, Six. Thank Uncle Nicolás again for my tuition money and clothes and stuff."

I wrapped my arms around her and kissed her. Tears streaked her smooth white cheeks. I dried them with my thumbs.

"What are me and Antonio going to do with the money Uncle Nicolás set aside? I don't need a degree to dig holes and prune tree limbs. That money's for you and José."

"Thank you, Six, for letting me follow my dream. Your trust is not misplaced. You'll be proud of me."

"I am already proud of you. You'll be the smartest astronomer that ever graduated from Columbia University, Hypatia. I'm sure of that."

I picked José up in my left arm. He was a compact little tyke for a four-year-old, his heft belying his size. Hypatia's friend Ginnie leaned on the horn. I walked her to the car. José waved at them as they drove away in Ginnie's sandblasted and sun-faded beater. We went back inside.

After setting José on the upholstered wooden booster Antonio had made for him and pulling him up to the table, I turned to the stove and heated rice and beans for our lunch.

I stirred it while keeping an eye on my son, which it still felt strange to say. Grandma had been dead a year and I missed her so terribly. But she lived on inside me and I still remembered what she taught me, especially how to make her special soup. I rolled the rice and beans into three tortillas and brought them to the table.

"I know you understand me, José , so let's not pretend. The first rule concerning your gifts is that you must never reveal them in the open. Right now that means only your Papa, no one else. Not your Mama or Tio Antonio, either. Running around upstairs and downstairs at the same time. You're gonna get caught some day."

José tried to stare me down, his eyes as deep as wells, dark and glistening. Then he looked away.

"Yes, Papa. I'll be good. Can I show my tarantula what I can do?"

"What tarantula?"

"Murphy," he said, placing the furry spider on the table, where it stopped, as though awaiting further instruction.

"How does a tarantula come by the name Murphy, José?"

"I found him at Mama's house hiding in the Murphy bed."

"Fair enough. And I know what you're going to ask. Tortillas are only for people."

"Yes, Papa. Can I make him bigger?"

"No. Most people don't like spiders."

"Why, Papa?"

"Beats me. Here. Have some more. We'll catch some flies for Murphy after we eat."

"Thank you, Papa. Can he sleep with you and Tio Antonio?"

"No."

"Why, Papa?"

"Too many legs in one bed. Murphy is your friend. Come on now. Down the chute."

He swallowed the rest of his tortilla and opened his mouth for a bite of mine.

"I'm making Grandma's soup tonight. If you're a good boy, you can have a sip, just a spoonful. And when you're a little older, José, I'll show you how she made it."

Murphy scrambled down his arm and disappeared under the table. I wasn't sure how Antonio felt about pet spiders, but I knew he'd do his best to spoil José as only an uncle could.

———————◦◦———————

José, now a strapping eleven-year-old, said no one from Mila-Grow Nursery & Greenhouse had dropped Antonio home after work. I'd been running errands all day in Española. I was worried, especially because he knew we were having my Grandma's soup and he never missed it. No one at work had a telephone, so all I could do was go look for Antonio.

Having learned to trust impressions and hunches over the years, I drove out to the West Rim where Antonio and I—and now José, too—often watched the sun set, The Gorge filling from bottom to top with darkness. He could have walked that far from Mila-Grow. I knew he'd had something heavy on his mind but he was not letting me in on it. Even José thought something was not right with his Tio Antonio.

The only light other than my headlights came from the full moon, circled by an icy halo, creeping over The Mountain. Our 1953 Ford pickup, which Antonio had sanded by hand and painted turquoise with a brush, bounced and swerved along the rutted road. The fans of illumination from the headlamps wavered and jounced in every direction, shining on sagebrush and leaning fenceposts as much as onto the road. It started snowing huge, wet flakes. The wipers barely kept up. I cranked up the heater. I was afraid I'd break an axle if I drove any faster.

The truck came to a stop near the outcrop where Antonio and I used to perch ourselves. He liked to go there sometimes to think. Antonio was outlined in the headlights, covered in snow. I reached the edge just as he leaped into empty space above The Gorge, eight hundred feet above the Rio Grande.

"Help me," he yelled, his voice resounding from the canyon walls. "Help me, Six."

I held Antonio suspended. He was light. He flailed in the air as though drowning. Little by little, his frantic arm and leg movements got him turned around and he continued as though swimming toward shore. When he was no longer hovering above

The Gorge, I grabbed his hand and let him float down beside me.

"Oh, Six. I'm so awful sorry. I regretted it as soon as I left the ground. Am I dreaming? Are you in my dream or am I in yours? Am I dead? What's happening, Six?"

"This is the true world, Antonio, part ordinary, part magic, part awake, part dreaming, all mixed together like my Grandma's soup."

Antonio sobbed into my shoulder, shaking. I trembled as badly as he did.

"My God, what were you thinking, Antonio? How did you ever come to such a desperate pass?"

"I'm so sorry, Six. I just couldn't live without you. I didn't think you'd stay when you found out what I'd done."

I kissed him and wrapped my arms around him. Then I walked him back to the pickup and helped him up into the cab. Melted snow dripped from his black hair. I backed up and headed down the bumpy road by which I'd come. The tire tracks were nearly filled in with fresh snow. I looked over at him quickly to gauge his expression.

"You saved my ass, buddy. You did a miracle, right?" Antonio asked.

"No, not really a miracle, just a gift I have. Now that we share a house and a bed, I do not want to have secrets from you any longer, Antonio. José can do certain things, too."

I saw him turn towards me, but I kept my eyes on the road.

"Six, I... I... um..."

"I know, Antonio. I could smell him on you, a smell that was not you."

The slushy snow was beginning to freeze. The wipers squeaked.

"Why didn't you tell me? Why couldn't you share your woe with me? I love you, Antonio. I forgive you even before you do something."

He snuffled and wiped his nose on his sleeve. I guessed he was crying but did not want to make a fuss about it. We continued on the way home in silence.

I pulled into our road. The warm glow from the steam-shrouded windows and the lazy twists of smoke from the chimney could not have looked more inviting.

"We won't say anything about any of this to José," I told him, "though I'd be surprised if he didn't suspect something was going on. He's a smart kid."

"Smarter than the two of us put together," Antonio added.

"Speak for yourself," I said, giving him a playful punch on the shoulder.

José flung open the kitchen door and ran out to throw his arms around his Tio Antonio's waist. The steam and aromas wafted around us. José had kept the soup simmering and had taken the bread from the oven. Having a boy's fleeting attention, he was not always so conscientious.

Antonio sat on the bench beside the kitchen door and tugged off his wet boots. He stripped to his longjohns and shirt, and stood next to the stove, toasting one side and then the other. I served three bowls of Grandma's soup and José sliced the bread, literally by hand, no knife. He turned to one side so Antonio would not see him.

"It's all right, José. Uncle Antonio knows what we can do. We don't have to hide our gifts when we are at home."

We sat down. I asked Antonio to say grace. He choked back tears.

"Bless all who gather at this table to partake of thy bounty, Lord. Bless Grandma's soup to our use and bless us to thy service. Amen."

José dove into his soup as though he'd fasted for days. Antonio was not far behind him. I smeared my jalapeño and cheddar bread with butter and watched them gobble up their soup.

"Does Hypatia know about your abilities?" Antonio asked, waiting to see who'd answer.

"No, Tio, Mama does not know; only Uncle Nicolás knows. In two years, when I'm thirteen, I'm going to live with Tio Nicolás and become his 'prentice just like Papa did."

"That's exciting news, José. Would you please pass the butter?"

José took a chunk of butter from the crock before sliding it across to Antonio.

"Tio Nicolás might teach me to fly."

Antonio seemed amused. I didn't think he quite believed what my son was telling him. But he'd catch on soon enough. At the bottom of his bowl were all three mushrooms, the first time Antonio would get the full magic, not just the broth. José certainly needed no magical encouragement.

After seconds of bread and soup all around, I sent Antonio upstairs to bed. José and I did dishes and stoked the stove. Then he went off to his room opposite the kitchen.

"Don't be up reading until dawn, José. We're going to church early tomorrow."

"Yes, Papa. I want to thank God for bringing Tio Antonio home safe."

"Good. Me, too," I said, giving him a squeeze and a kiss good-night.

Upstairs, Antonio sat in his longjohns at the edge of the bed, the covers pulled back. He turned and smiled. I could see his breath by the light of the old railroad lantern on the dresser.

"What are you waiting for?" I asked him. "It's freezing up here. Climb in, buddy."

"I feel so strange, Six, like my eyes are open all the way instead of half-closed."

"That's Grandma's soup, Antonio. You got all her special mushrooms this time. It will wear off. I wanted you to learn about the magic there is all around us. Don't be afraid. I love you."

I tugged off my boots and scrambled out of my clothes, getting completely naked, ready to climb in. Antonio took hold of my shoulders and raised me to my feet, drawing me to him, chest-to-chest, his arms around my waist. He hugged me so hard I could barely breathe.

"I love you, too, Six. You are my life."

He continued pulling me closer until there was no room between us, and he pulled some more. I was partly inside him, and he in me, arms and legs and torsos entwined, two bodies occupying one space.

I glanced at us in the dresser mirror. We looked like a

double-exposure. Only our heads remained independent. I probably had as much Spanish blood in me as Antonio, but his other half was Indian; mine was Norwegian. Antonio turned to look in the mirror, too.

"This is your magic, Antonio. I'm not doing anything except getting cold."

We stepped away from each other. We'd gotten so close to one another I was now wearing Antonio's longjohns, only they were on backwards. He laughed and I pulled them off. We tumbled onto the bed and scrambled beneath the covers.

We'd just gotten settled in, lying next to each other for warmth and solace, when I saw the shadow of Murphy, amplified by the lamplight, amble across the quilt. Antonio stretched out his arm to the tarantula, and tickled the fur on its back.

"OK, Murphy. Better get back to José's room," he told the spider. "He'll be missing you come morning. It turns out we've got enough legs in bed after all. Good night."

We watched Murphy's gigantic shadow retreat.

I recalled Uncle Nicolás advising me, *It is often best to do healing in dreams so no one remembers you were there.* I wanted to heal Antonio's hurt and woe, and hoped he'd forgive himself.

I turned my head and kissed his shoulder. Slipping down into sleep beside him, I joined him in his dream, my arms wide open as he walked toward me among the snow-flocked sagebrush. He carried a wicker basket of red mushrooms with white spots, the kind in my Grandma's soup. His eyes and smile glistened in the moonlight as he offered me the basket.

CAMERA OBSCURA

I sit down at the edge of the bed. The mattress sags, the springs squeak, and the brass bedstead raps against the wall. My husband opens his eyes. They are cloudy, his look far-off. Perhaps he does not see me. I rest my hand on his hands, folded atop the sheet and threadbare quilt. His fingers are gnarled like the roots of an old cottonwood, his skin rough as bark. Sixtus responds to my touch by looking up into my eyes, his gaze now focused and piercing, a blue like melting ice.

"Are you hungry, Sixtus?" I ask him. "I've brought you some soup."

His eyes brighten and he props himself up on his elbow, waiting for me to pile pillows behind him. When he is settled, I turn up the old kerosene lantern and reach for the bowl and spoon on the night table. Tucking the napkin under his chin, I scrape my knuckles on his stubbly skin. I put the spoon to his lips.

"Ah," he says in a rasp. "Your mushroom soup."

"I thought it might calm you."

"Do I appear agitated, my dear?"

"Fifty years is not enough time to learn you," I tell him. "I still can't read your face."

"Bemused, dear Anna. My expression is always bemused, *risado*."

"When you are finished, maybe I can bring a pan of warm water and help you shave," I remark, pouring another spoonful of soup into his mouth before he can sass me.

He swallows with difficulty. A dribble courses down among his whiskers.

"Let the undertaker take care of making me presentable."

"Sixtus. Stop it. I don't like that kind of dreary talk."

"We both know where this is headed, my dear. I'm ready. My only regret is that I will not live to see *mi amado bisnieto*, my great-grandson, the one who will next receive our family gift."

"Perhaps the mushrooms will bring you a dream tonight. But you must finish the soup."

He grins and opens his mouth. He soon polishes off the rest of the bowl, but there is more soup on his napkin and in his whiskers than made it past his lips. I turn down the old railroad lantern from his years working on the Cumbres & Toltec line. Before I have reached the bedroom door, he snores with a noise like sawing wood. I can wish for nothing better than that my soup will provide my husband a vision, a vision of the world he will never see. I hope it comforts him.

Taking the bowl and spoon to the kitchen downstairs, I draw water from the pump at the sink. I push the kettle of soup onto the drainboard to cool. Two tears I cannot contain spatter down onto the stove, sizzling and dancing their brief lives away.

I lie down on the settee in the parlor and cover myself with an afghan my mother knitted as our wedding present. It needs mending. Closing my eyes, I pray that I will receive my own dream. How shall I let my husband of more than a half-century leave me forever? I pray for help.

I can see our great-grandson clearly in my dreams, but I want to show my Sixtus what the boy looks like. I have tried many times, but I'm unable to carry my husband's Kodak brownie with me into the future to snap our great-grandson's photo. I am no artist, either, and cannot draw the boy as he appears to me. I am afraid Sixtus will be gone before I can learn the right magic. I fear he will die soon.

That night a dream comes to me. I am visited by an ancestor

of mine from the Fifteenth Century, an artist from Valencia. Francisco is dressed in fine silk clothing, a successful artist who has passed his magical gifts down to me but none of his artistic talents or skills. I ask him if there is some way to show a picture of our *bisnieto* to my husband.

Francisco tells me about the *cámara oscura*, a technique for projecting an image onto the wall of a darkened room. I ask him whether it is magic.

"No, Señora, it was discovered by an ordinary man, an Italian from whom I learned the device. I shall tell you what you must do so that your husband will be able to see your great-grandson. Your beloved will die peacefully."

"Gratias, Señor Francisco. I fear my husband has become bitter because the gift has passed him by and come to me—oh, so many years ago. My dear Sixtus thinks the gift ought to pass only to the men in is own lineage. I want him to forgive me."

"The gift passes back and forth among several lineages. It chooses whom it will, Señora Anna. The magic is uncountably old. It does not come as a favor from faraway gods high above. It is born of the earth; it comes from itself and serves itself. We are merely vessels."

"Yes, I understand. Please pray for my husband."

"I have, dearest Anna. Your husband will forgive you and die satisfied. Rest your mind."

Francisco de Orsona takes my hand and smiles. All the lamps in his studio dim. I feel his grasp slip away, and I pass over into an unremarkable dream, one I do not remember.

———————❍———————

I awaken clutching the carved armrest of the old settee. There is a crick in my neck but a lightness in my heart.

As I sit up and walk stiffly to the kitchen, Sixtus calls for me. At least I know he has made it through the night. I have one chance still to show him our great-grandson.

I climb the stairs. He has filled the bedpan to near overflowing. He sheepishly averts his gaze.

"I am sorry, my dearest Anna, that it has come to this, as though I were a child once again, unable to care for himself. But I won't be a bother much longer."

Choosing not to respond, I pour the contents of the bedpan into the chamber pot.

"I'm afraid, my dear," I say to him, "that for the first time in memory, I've run out of oatmeal for your breakfast. Little Adám doesn't deliver our way again until Friday. I'm sorry, Sixtus. Especially now when I want to make you comfortable."

"That's all right," he tells me, the blue ice in his eyes catching the glint of bright sunlight. "I never much cared for oatmeal anyway."

After all our years together, I still don't know when he's joshing me or telling me what he means. He keeps me on my toes, even now in his last days.

"I received a dream last night, Sixtus, a way to show you our great-grandson."

His eyes flash surprise, but he does not say anything.

I bring soap and hot water and his razor from the privy downstairs. Then I place a towel across his chest. He heaves with coughing. I wait for the spasms to subside, afraid I will cut him.

"You must be handsome when you meet the boy," I tell him.

"Yes, Anna. You have subdued me once again with your sweet talk."

Certain he will not believe me, I do not tell my husband my magic is an ordinary trick of optics, as Francisco explained to me. Our great-grandson will be standing in our side yard in the bright morning sun, twelve years into the future. The boy's image will shine onto the wall of our bedroom like a picture from a movie projector.

When I have finished, I gather the shaving gear and help Sixtus into a fresh shirt. His arms and chest are so thin it fits him like someone else's shirt. I prop the pillows behind him so he sits as straight as possible. Then I draw down the heavy green window shades.

"What're you doing, my dear? How am I supposed to see the next Sixtus in our family in a darkened room?"

His voice is weak and interrupted by rasping and wheezing.

"This is how the magic was explained to me. Be patient."

I wait for the chiming clock on the sideboard downstairs to sound nine o'clock. Taking a thick pin from my apron, I poke a hole in the window shade opposite the empty wall beside the dresser. A shaft of sunlight on which dust motes swirl and dance shines onto the plaster wall.

"Why's the boy standing on his head? He work for the circus or something?" Sixtus asks, sounding more amused than annoyed.

"I don't know, dear. I must've remembered the instructions in the dream wrong."

"You've made a camera obscura, Anna, a discovery from the Renaissance to help artists with the principles of perspective. It's not magic, dear."

"No?" I ask him, annoyed at his comments. "You're watching someone not yet born who won't be standing in our yard for a dozen more years. That's not magic?"

"Well, I'll give you that, Anna. Please bring my Papa's lantern from downstairs."

"Why, Sixtus? I was told the room has to be dark."

"I don't want to watch *mi bisnieto* upside down. It makes my head dizzy."

I fetch the lantern from the sideboard in the kitchen. It is so old it does not even burn kerosene but uses a thick plumber's candle. The four heavy glass sides are beveled and faceted. A circular lens is at the heart of each pane.

Steadying the lantern in his lap, I watch him slide one of the glass sides past the metal brackets that hold it in place. He lifts the pane out through the hinged lid of the lantern. I set the lantern on the floor and turn down the kerosene lamp on the dresser.

Sitting on the bed beside Sixtus, I lean forward to watch our *bisnieto*, now right-side up, through the lantern lens. My husband is so clever. I wonder, if he hadn't been so headstrong, whether the gift might have gone to him. He would have made a powerful *brujo*, maybe stronger than me.

The boy will be the next Sixtus in the family. He will be the one to whom I will pass the family gift, bypassing our children and all their children. He likes to be called just "Six." He mouths the words I have told him to say, and I recite them for my husband.

"Bless you, Great-grandfather, *mi bisabuelo*. I am Six, your great-grandson from 1960."

The boy was not saying what we'd rehearsed back in the future. I had told him to say his full name, Sixtus van Thorson, like his great-grandfather's.

"How wonderful, my boy. Bless you, too. Who's the president these days?"

"Quiet, Sixtus," I tell my husband. "You're supposed to just listen. It's not a walkie-talkie. Let the boy speak."

"General Eisenhower is president," our great-grandson says, not following the script.

I am not sure how the boy is able to talk to us across time, from the future. He was supposed to just mouth the words we'd practiced.

"I'm happy for that. He's an honorable man, a good man," my husband says.

"Don't you two have anything better to discuss than politics?" I ask them.

"That's what men do, Anna: discuss politics. And women's hemlines."

" Shush, Sixtus. You're a bad example."

"At least I'm an honest bad example," he says, choking on his joke. The coughing continues.

I am certain the magic that lets them speak back-and-forth across time is not mine. I do not think my husband can do more than sending and receiving thoughts. The magic must be the boy's. What, I wonder, will he able to do when he has grown to manhood?

I turn up the railroad lantern and pour Sixtus a glass of water, hoping his coughing will subside. The image of out great-grandson fades in even that dim, flickering light. There is a dribble of blood on my husband's chin and a spot on his clean shirt.

Leaning over to rest my hand on his chest, I look into my husband's eyes. Once again his gaze is cloudy and far away. His chest heaves up and down as he struggles to breathe. I realize he is leaving me. *No*, I think. *I am not ready to say Good-bye. Two more days.*

"Go to your rest, *mi bisabuelo*," the boy Six says. "I love you. The world is better for your having walked upon it. Your love lives with us. Good-night, Great-grandfather."

Then the boy turns to look at me.

"Please do not fret, Great-grandmother. Before my great-grandfather left this world, while you fetched his lantern, he asked me to tell you his final thoughts, his last wishes.

"He said you must ease your mind. He forgives you even though there is nothing to forgive. The gift came to you because you were the most worthy, just like it will skip two generations and come to our great-grandson.

"If I find my way to an afterlife, I will love you there like I do here for as long as that lasts. Good-bye, my dearest."

The window shade flaps up with a noise like startled crows in a barn loft. I nearly jump out of my skin. The boy's image vanishes the instant sunlight pours into the room.

I throw myself across my husband's chest, now motionless, as though my mere mortal weight could hold back a soul on its journey. I embrace Sixtus, but he is gone. My flood of tears spills into the gullies and arroyos of his wrinkled neck.

Sixtus still looks at the place on the wall where our *bisnieto* stood. I close his eyes and leave the room. I will walk to the neighbor's to use her telephone, but first I need to sit down.

Once my great-grandson was born and we lived in the same town and time, it became easier to talk, though he did not always pay attention. He had an independent streak like my Sixtus and like my son Nicolás. But he was a good boy and a handsome boy and a worthy recipient of our family gifts.

I was sorry Six would not ever get married, but in my dreams I know he has a son. I know that sometimes happens. God works his mysteries and I do not question them. Since I cannot picture the boy's face, my great-great grandson, I know I must be leaving the world before he arrives. His name does not come to me, either.

Six knocks on the bedroom door before coming in. At thirteen, he is growing into manhood. I see my husband's look-alike standing before me, lanky and slightly awkward. Six comes twice a week to read to me. I am blind in one eye and cannot see well with the other.

"I am sorry, dear boy," I tell him. "I do not feel so good today. My strength has left me. I am sorry you've come all this way. We'll have to leave the conclusion of *A Wrinkle in Time* until later. Just sit here with me and hold my hand. I am cold."

"*Si, mi bisabuela,*" he says.

I feel his warmth and strength—and his power.

"I think I will shut my eyes and have a short nap," I tell him.

"Yes, Great-grandma," he replies, his voice soothing, trailing far away. "You have a little nap. I'll come back to finish the book tomorrow."

———————◦———————

"I did not mean to trick you, *bisabuela,*" I say to her corpse. "I led you to be believe we would finish the book. I did not want you to fret about your last day. Death came for you today, when you did not expect him. Go now to your rest, and be with *mi bisabuelo.*"

I extinguish the old kerosene lantern and roll up the heavy green window shade with the hole in it. Sunlight washes into the room in a blinding dazzle. I lean over my great-grandmother and kiss her forehead. Then I leave the bedroom.

In the hallway, in the *nicho,* is her favorite icon of "The Gifts of the Magi" in which three wise men, kings of the East, lay their presents before the Holy Family, Jesús, Maria and José, in the stable. The image was painted on wood by a long-ago ancestor in Spain. The picture was my great-grandma's most treasured possession.

I touch the old painting, holding back tears that burst forth anyhow. Then I blow out the votive candle in the *nicho* and leave my great-grandparents' house for the last time.

LIKE FATHER, LIKE SON

José and his father, Sixtus, meander through the woods behind their adobe *casita* following well-worn deer paths. The trail winds in many directions before opening onto the meadow and the *acequia* that brings water to everything on their *ranchito*.

The sun is intense this spring afternoon. New leaves only emerging, the aspen grove offers no shade. A late winter chill hugs the ground and flies upward with the gusts of wind. The ground is damp enough that the wind raises no dust.

They follow the portion of the *acequia* that flows through their ten acres and the neighbor's five, estimating how much work will be entailed in clearing the winter debris from the watercourse. José jots notes his father dictates in a small notebook he keeps in the pocket of his denim workshirt. His Levi's are wet and muddy from trying to clear a leaf-dam with a branch. The water is as cold as the spring melt that feeds it.

"I told you this was just a survey, José. Now you get to squish all the way home."

"I know, but I figured if I cleared that stretch a little, the extra flow might carry most of the leaves and blockage downstream where it'd be someone else's problem."

"That's not how taking care of the *acequias* works, son. If our neighbors felt that way, the water would stop in no time. Instead, the water has been flowing for three hundred years, bringing life to most of this valley."

Sixtus, whom everyone calls Six, notices when his son's

boots and jeans stop squelching. He sees they are a lighter color again and perfectly dry.

"No using magic to dry out your clothes, José," he tells the teenager. "When you do something stupid, there are results. When you fall in water you get wet. Now go get wet again."

"Papa. It's freezing."

"You know magic is not for your benefit or mine. It's to help the people who need us."

The sixteen-year-old looks like neither his fair-skinned, blue-eyed mother nor his auburn-haired, green-eyed father. He has the features and coloring of the Spanish side of the family rather than the Norwegian side which Six resembles.

José takes a running jump into the icy watercourse, emerging with his blue-black hair plastered to his skull like a glistening coat of paint. He puffs and blows to get his breath, and scrambles back up the embankment. Six shivers looking at his son and decides to cut their expedition short. Father and son head back across the meadow toward the woods.

"There are some who might say making me walk home in wet clothes is mistreating a child," José tells his father.

Six stops in his tracks and glares at him.

"First of all, you're no longer a child. Secondly, I didn't push you into the water. You chose to jump."

"Yeah, like Tio Antonio," the teenager retorts, aware what a hurtful thing it was to say after his Uncle Antonio's suicide.

Six uses all the magic he knows and all the self-control he possesses to keep from striking the boy across the mouth. He raises his arms and directs his fury into his fingertips, from which tines of white-hot lightning strike the ground. Dirt and stones and tufts of grass shoot upwards, leaving small craters in the damp ground. José's wet clothes are dried instantly on the front side which faced the incandescent flash. The boy is speechless.

Father and son continue on their way across the meadow and back into the woods in silence. Six knows his display of anger at the boy's remark did not set a good example, but José also knows how to elicit that reaction. Six wonders if it isn't a game they play. The teenager could not have hurt his father if Six hadn't pondered endlessly what he could have done differently to keep his partner, Antonio, from leaping off a cliff into The Gorge that past winter. *No, I didn't push Antonio, but by getting there ten seconds too late, I may as well have.*

Six realizes the boy misses his Tio Antonio, too, having grown up with his "two papas" since he was a toddler. Both their wounds are fresh. He forgives his son for his hurtful remark, and places his hand on his shoulder as they cross the yard to the *casita*. José does not pull away as he sometimes does, but accepts the gesture.

The lanky teenager rushes inside and stands with his damp backside to the woodstove. Six smiles at him.

In the same instant, both father and son begin to say, "I'm sorry..."

They laugh.

"I thought we'd make my grandma's soup tonight, José. I want you to learn how to make it and what it's good for."

"Terrific. It's my favorite."

"Mine, too," Six replies. "And maybe some jalepeño and cheddar bread. I think you'll have to bring in more wood. Feels like it will fall below freezing again tonight."

"Sure, Papa. Can I finish drying out first?"

Six nods and José pats himself to see where he still needs to toast himself. He discovers the sodden notebook in his shirt pocket and flips it open. All the ink has smeared; his notes are illegible. He shows it to his father who at first looks crestfallen but manages to smile.

"*When you do something stupid, there are results,*" José says, quoting his father.

"And not only for the person who's not thinking," Six remarks. "Come here, son."

Six enfolds the boy in a hug, which José returns. The boy's head reaches Six's chin. *When did that happen?* Six wonders.

José goes to the barn for two armloads of wood for the stove. Six lays out the vegetables on the cutting board and drops two big beef bones into the pot of swirling water, remembering the time his grandmother taught him how to make her magic mushroom soup.

———————————◗◦◖———————————

Summer passes without father and son getting into any serious arguments. They have enough chores on their little ranch to think of little else. But once school starts again, José resumes his surly attitude. By the start of winter, when they spend most of their time indoors, clashes between Six and José are a daily occurrence.

"When is Mama going to get here? I'm starving," José complains to his father.

"You're always hungry. You must have hollow legs. Your mother will get here about the time her friend Ginnie's beater delivers her to our door. The roads are crowded on Thanksgiving.

"If you'd concentrate a little, José, you might be able to see ahead a couple hours and not always be asking me. You keep peeling potatoes, all right? Just in case she gets here on time. I'm going to bring in more wood and close up the barn."

The truculent teenager watches his father from the kitchen window. It is snowing. His mother will be even later. He is ready to chomp down on the raw potato in his hand.

The front door, which José and Six never use, bursts open as from a gust of wind. Hypatia blows in as a force of nature, her hair flung in all directions and trailing billows of snow.

"Mama. You got here early," José says, dropping the potato and peeler into the sink, and rushing to hug and kiss her.

"Ginnie had some party she didn't want to be late for. Her driving scared the bejesus out of me, José. Where's your father?"

"Bringing in more wood."

She rustles his thick black hair and smiles at him.

"Do you think you could maybe call me *Mom*, José? Mama makes me feel old, you know, like *I Remember Mama* on TV."

"We don't have TV, Mama."

"You're not getting the message, either, José."

"Sorry... *Mom*. And what do I call Papa?"

"Whatever he answers to, I guess," she tells her son, laughing. "I just don't want to be called anyone's *Mama*."

"Not even mine?"

"Oh, of course, dear boy. I'm sorry. Come here," Hypatia says, drawing him to her again. "I'll make an exception in your case. But you're the only person in the world who's allowed to call me *Mama*."

Six, arms laden with firewood, kicks open the kitchen door with the toe of his boot and pushes it closed with the heel. His hair and shoulders are frosted with light, fluffy snow that melts as soon as he draws near the stove. He drops his bundle into the tinder box with a clatter and embraces Hypatia.

"What smells so good?" Hypatia asks Six, kissing him.

"It's either me or the stuffed chicken."

She tickles his ribs and he squirms out of reach.

"I've still got to slice the potatoes and grate the cheese and get the pan of scalloped potatoes in the oven."

"I can do that, Six. José and I have catching up to do. Would you mind putting my bags upstairs? They're out on the front porch."

Six stands in the open doorway for a moment surveying the array of luggage before picking up the two largest suitcases. He brushes the snow off of them.

"What's in these? Bricks?" Six asks, again kicking the door shut with his boot.

"I've got reading to catch up on before my interview in Flagstaff next week. Astronomy books are as heavy as their subject matter."

Six takes the suitcases one at a time upstairs to his and Antonio's bedroom—to *his* bedroom now. He finds himself getting choked up and sits at the edge of the bed to regain control. He doesn't want Hypatia to feel glum on his account.

Downstairs, Hypatia and José peel and slice and grate. After putting the baking dish of scalloped potatoes on the lower rack in the oven, Hypatia slides the chicken on the upper rack forward and bastes it. She grabs a towel and yanks off the two wings, which she and José devour.

"Are you and Papa getting back together?" José asks her, gnawing every last morsel off the bones.

"It looks that way, doesn't it?" Hypatia chuckles. "We were

never really together, José. After I had you, I stayed with Ginnie's family and finished high school. Your papa went to live with his Uncle Nicolás. Then he moved into this house with your Uncle Antonio."

Six hears his friend's name as he descends the stairs. He wonders what his son and the boy's mother have been talking about. He goes around the house from the kitchen door this time in order to get a larger dose of fresh air. The door closes softly and mother and son resume their conversation.

"I loved your father for his body; he loved me for my mind. We love each other very much, José, just not in the same way."

"Will I be as screwed up as most of the adults I know?" José asks his mother.

"Probably. But don't worry. Nearly all of it comes naturally."

They burst into laughter just as Six enters with the rest of Hypatia's baggage. He decides he's happy Hypatia and their son are enjoying each other's company at Thanksgiving. Six hopes he can join them in their good mood.

"The smaller bag can stay down here, Six. It's just my bath-room things."

"Yes, ma'am," he tells her, setting the overnight bag down and holding out his hand as though for a tip.

Hypatia places her gnawed wing bone in his open palm. The three of them laugh and huddle closer to the stove.

"Would you care for a beer, Hypatia?" Six asks.

"Yes, please."

"Waiter," Six says to José. "Please bring us three beers."

"Three?"

"You heard your papa. Three beers."

They sit at the kitchen table which José has set for their Thanksgiving supper—three places as he is used to. José snaps the caps off the bottles and they clink them together.

"I want to let you both know that I've also applied to Cambridge," Hypatia announces. "I was alerted to a teaching position there by my friend and colleague Professor Hawking."

"You mean like in England?" José asks.

"Your visits will be even rarer," Six protests. "Aren't the

night skies clear enough here in old Red Willow?"

"Yes, they are, but the nearest large observatory is in Flag-staff. That's why I applied there, too," Hypatia tells them, taking a long swallow of her beer. She is way ahead of Six and José.

"I hope you get the job in Arizona," José tells her.

"We'll see. I have done all I can to land both positions. It's no longer in my hands."

Six and Hypatia enjoy a second beer while José nurses his first and last. They continue their conversation which winds around and gets tangled in knots. The ding of the oven timer startles them all.

"I think our supper should be ready," Six announces. "José, please give me a hand."

"I can help, too," Hypatia says.

"I think Mama just wants to snatch some food."

"I believe you're right, José. Should we let her?"

Hypatia slaps both their behinds. "Like father, like son," she tells them.

They each manage to pinch a few morsels while getting the food from the oven and the stove onto the platter and into bowls. They lick their fingers and smack their lips as though table manners applied only when they were at the table.

They stand at their places, their hands resting on the backs of their chairs.

"Mama, will you say our grace?"

Hypatia is startled by the request. She mostly does not believe in God, while Six and José—and Antonio when he was alive—attend mass every Sunday and holy day. She clears her throat.

"God bless the food we are about to share. We are grateful for the blessing in our lives of Antonio's love, whose spirit partakes with us tonight."

First José, and then Six, caught unaware by her beautiful prayer, allow tears to stream down their faces unashamedly. They leave their places and enfold one another, sobbing openly. Hypatia joins them, taking her place between father and son.

José steals glances over his shoulder at the steaming, beck-

204 • BRIAN ALLAN SKINNER

oning meal they have prepared. His stomach rumbles and they all smile. The family take their seats at the table, each looking over, every now and again, at the empty fourth chair where Antonio usually sat.

———————◦◦◦———————

Six sleeps cramped and curled up on the sagging settee near the front door. Antonio comes to him in a dream. Six does not trust dreams. Antonio looks as handsome as his usual self, but it's hard for Six to look at him directly. Everything is so bright.

"My God, Antonio," Six says, his voice trembling. "Is it really you? Why did you do it? Why did you leave me? My heart is broken, buddy."

"I am so sorry, Six. I repented the instant my feet left the cliff. And I'm especially sorry for hurting little José. I didn't think far enough. I stopped thinking at the edge of The Gorge. I was afraid you'd leave me after I cheated on you and I couldn't live without you."

"It hasn't been a picnic without you, either, you know. I smelled the other guy on you, Antonio. But I love you and would forgive anything you did. Please, help me with José. He looked up to you. You were his second papa."

"I will, Six," Antonio tells him. "Actually, I was sent. I have to help save someone else in order to save myself. I'm not supposed to tell you this, but everyone gets saved in the end. Some of us have to work harder at it than others. I'm here to help with José."

"I need all the help I can get, Antonio. That boy goes out of his way to say hurtful things to me. I know he blames me for not saving you. He never brings his friends around, either, like he's ashamed of me."

"Maybe it's his chums he's ashamed of. He so wants to be like them, Six, but he is so much better."

"Any ideas what I can do? I'm afraid Hypatia and I are going to lose him. I miss your advice, Antonio."

"You got it, buddy. It's time for me to make up for some of

the damage I've done. I'll do all I can to protect José, sort of like a Guardian Uncle. You'll get a few pointers on what to do in the next dream coming up."

"Let me kiss you good-bye, Antonio. I never got to do that."

Six wraps his arms around his friend. Antonio feels real but insubstantial. He kisses him and looks in his eyes. Antonio grows dimmer and fuzzier until Six is once more alone. He awakens unwillingly and struggles to regain sleep.

He wakes up the second time stiff and aching. He wonders how he will last another two weeks on the cramped, lumpy settee while Hypatia visits them. He smells bacon and flapjacks. Slipping on his Levi's, he goes to investigate. It is not Hypatia standing at the stove as he expected, but rather José.

"Are you trying to butter me up for something, kiddo?" Six asks him.

"No, I want to butter Mama up. I want to go with her to Santa Fe, today. Can I, Papa? Please."

"I thought we'd go see Tio Antonio today."

The boy pours his father a cup of coffee from the speckled enamel pot.

"Can't we go on Sunday when Mama and me get back? Mama will be going to England soon and it'll be a long time before I see her again."

"You saw this? You know this, José? She's going to get the job in England, not Arizona?"

The boy nods. "I miss her already."

Six tousles his son's hair. He wants to give him a hug, but the teenager is busy flipping several flapjacks at once like a juggler. Six wants to again counsel him against doing magic openly, but he decides to go easy on him.

"If your mama says it's OK, then it's all right with me."

The boy turns around to hug his father.

"No magic, José. Your mama gets very uncomfortable around things she can't explain. There's no reason for her to know what you can do. She loves you very much anyway. I'm going upstairs to awaken her."

"All right," José says. "Breakfast will be ready."

As Six ascends the stairs, José quickly adds kindling and a pair of logs to the stove and strikes a match. José had been cooking without fire, something he'd been warned never to do in front of anyone except his father and his Tio Antonio.

<hr>

Hypatia and José drive to Santa Fe in Six's old Ford pickup that Antonio hand-sanded and painted turquoise with a brush.

After work, Six sits at the kitchen table and watches the daylight fade, the last streaks of rose and gold sinking behind The Mountain. It is his first night alone in the house since Antonio died a year ago. The house feels empty, cold, and much too quiet. He thinks of having a couple shots of tequila, but does not want to console himself in that way. Instead he goes to the barn to bring in a load of firewood.

When he returns, his great-uncle, Tio Nicolás, is sitting at the kitchen table, where he has set out two shot glasses and a bottle of tequila. Six drops the wood into the tinder box. He is surprised to see Tio Nicolás, though he has been thinking about him lately.

"Sit down, Nephew. I know you've been wanting to talk to me."

"Are you the dream I was told to expect? Am I dreaming, Tio?"

"What do you think?" Nicolás asks, pouring tequila into each of the small glasses and sliding one across the table to his great-nephew. "A dream... a visit... What's the difference so long as you get the message?"

"What message is that, Tio?"

"That you need to go easier on yourself," Nicolás says.

He lifts his shot glass and urges Six to do the same. They swallow their tequila and Tio Nicolás refills the glasses.

"Yes, you forgive Antonio for what he did, but you have not forgiven yourself for not reaching him in time. It is not your fault. Forgive yourself at mass this Sunday. And forgive José for being hard on you. He is doing his best, too. He struggles to stay afloat. You and the boy lock horns because you are alike. You are both *testarudo*, stubborn."

Nicolás raises his shot glass of tequila.

"Here, Nephew. Let's drink to the boy's education," he toasts. "Perhaps it is time for him to come live with me and become my apprentice as you did. What do you think, Six?"

"I will miss him so much. The house will be empty, Tio. But I know it's best for José. I'll talk it over with Hypatia before she has to go back to New York in two weeks. It will take a lot to convince her."

"You speak very well, Nephew," the old man says, smiling. "Hypatia will see it your way. José is such a lucky boy: two papas, a beautiful mama, and now his Tio Nicolás. He will be unable to contain his joy."

———◦———

While Six and his great-uncle discuss what to do about José at the kitchen table, José and his mother wait for her friend Ginnie to close her shop in Santa Fe. The teenager taps his foot and fidgets with the racks of her ugly and expensive turquoise jewelry.

At last the final customer leaves. Ginnie grabs her coat and turns out the lights.

"Are we going out to eat now, Mom?" José asks. "I'm starving."

"You must have hollow legs," his mother remarks.

"Mind if we go next door for a little drinkie first?" Ginnie asks, turning the key in the lock.

Hypatia and José accompany her down the street to her favorite after-work hangout, The Ornery Burro. To José's dismay, "next door" is at the end of the block.

At the bar, a fellow lies passed-out on the floor. They step around him.

"I'll have what he's having," Ginnie tells the bartender, pointing to the man on the floor.

"You probably couldn't afford it, Ginnie. He likes fancy vodka imported from Russia. Here. Take a look," Lloyd says, showing them the bottle.

"Let me see," Hypatia says. "I know a little Russian. It was a collaboration debunking the crackpot theories of Velikovsky."

He turns the bottle with the fancy silver-and-blue label toward Hypatia. She laughs.

"*Fonarnoye Toplivo* translates as *Lantern Fuel*," she tells them.

"Mind if I see some identification?" Lloyd tells Hypatia.

Hypatia smiles, and blushes a little. She withdraws her wallet from her purse and produces her New York State driver's license.

"Hypatia Diggs. Wow. The famous astronomer. I read about you in *Scientific American*."

"You read *Scientific American*?" Hypatia asks him.

"Why not? My wife got me the subscription for Christmas."

It is clear from his expression and his aloof stance that José is as bored as it's possible for a teenager to be. It seems he would rather not be seen with his mother and her friend. He begs Hypatia for quarters for the jukebox and she obliges happily.

José regrets his decision to go with his mother to Santa Fe. They've had little time to talk. He annoys the patrons of The Ornery Burro by playing the most raucous rock 'n' roll tunes he can find. Back home in Red Willow José's father and great-great uncle discuss the boy's future.

"Come, Nephew. Let's go for a walk," Tio Nicolás says. "We will come back and stand by the stove and maybe have a nightcap."

They put on their warm jackets hanging on pegs by the back door, and slip on their gloves. Neither wears a cap or hat.

"I am worried about José, Uncle. He's a good boy, but I think his friends are not a good influence. He'd rather be ordinary like them. He does not study his magic, thinking he can do things without practice. You and I know it will get him into trouble."

Six's cowboy boots and Uncle Nicolás's moccasins crunch on the ice-crusted snow. Their breath hangs in clouds that billow behind them. The trail through the woods is brilliantly lit by the full moon. When the path narrows, Six permits his great-uncle to walk first. It is a starry, crystalline night.

"Antonio came to me in a dream last night, Tio."

"Yes, I know. He was sent. I promised to help."

"What don't you know, Uncle?" Six asks him.

"About ninety-eight-and-a-half percent," he replies.

Uncle Nicolás stoops over near the trunk of a towering cottonwood. He brushes aside the glistening snow with his bare fingers and picks a small green plant, like tangled lavender, from among the winding roots.

"There's an herb for every situation and condition," Nicolás explains. "You must put this in a small plastic bag and hide it in José's pocket before school."

"But what if my son gets caught with it? Everyone will thinks it's..."

"Of course they will, and so will his friends. They'll think José is holding out on them and snatch the herb from him. They'll probably smoke it in the alley behind the school."

They turn back at the edge of the woods before it opens up on the meadow where the snow is deeper. They follow their footprints back home.

"Do you think that will be enough to do the trick, Tio Nicolás?"

"You wait and see," he reassures his nephew. "It's not called *stinkwort* for nothing."

———◦———

By seven o'clock, José is famished. He annoys the patrons of The Ornery Burro with his choice of music. His mother and her friend are on their third glasses of *Lantern Fuel* and orange juice. They bother those who haven't already left with their loud laughter. Even the fellow on the floor has crawled off.

At last, Hypatia, Ginnie, and José have the entire bar to

themselves. Lloyd does not appear to be as amused with them as they are with themselves. José asks for another orange juice and a third bag of pretzels, his only supper. Hypatia notices him towering over her.

"Don't stand on the stool, dear," she tells him. "People sit there with their nice clothes."

"I'm not on the stool, Mama."

She and Ginnie see that José is floating three feet off the floor. Their mouths drop open. Ginnie screams. The bartender looks over the bar to see what is going on.

"My God! José! What are you doing? That's not possible," his mother tells him.

José floats a mere couple of inches from the pressed-tin ceiling. The bartender tries to hand the bag of pretzels up to him. His arm is not long enough.

"That's a pretty neat trick, kid. How do you do that?" Lloyd asks the boy.

"It's not a trick," he explains. "It's magic."

"Are we dreaming?" Ginnie asks her friend. "What José is doing is just plain old impossible, isn't it?"

"You're right," Hypatia exclaims. "You can't do that, José. Get down here. I won't tell you again."

José spins himself around, tumbling and turning as though on a trapeze. The three adults watch him with their mouths agape. Ginnie applauds. The twirling teenager descends to the wood floor. His mother swats his behind.

Hypatia gestures to Ginnie to come along, but her friend ignores it.

"Let's have another round, Lloyd," Ginnie tells the bartender.

"Don't you think you've had enough Russian vodka for one night?" he asks her. "We're all seeing things. Get that crazy kid outta here."

"But you don't drink, Lloyd," Ginnie reminds him. "But you saw José twirling, too, didn't you?"

"I think we'll take your suggestion, Lloyd, and bid you a good night," Hypatia announces, tugging on Ginnie's sleeve.

The two women are a little unsteady and they each latch

onto one of José's elbows. The trio go out the door sideways. The sidewalk is just wide enough for them without uncoupling.

It is determined José would be the safest driver. Though he does not yet have his driver's license, Six has been giving him lessons. Ginnie's apartment is only a half-mile off Cerrillos. Hypatia hands her son the keys. She and Ginnie plop onto the back seat, giggling like schoolgirls.

"Oh, brother," José remarks, starting the engine and adjusting the rearview mirror.

He pulls away from the curb. There is more laughter from the back. Ginnie leans over the front seat to tell José where next to turn. She screams.

"What?" Hypatia hollers, lurching forward and hanging over the seat. She screams.

"José, you get back on the driver's side this instant. There's nobody driving the car. That's not safe."

"I'm driving the car, Mama."

"Then act like it. Scoot over to the driver's side and put your hands on the wheel and your feet on the pedals."

"I've done OK so far, haven't I?"

"That's not the point," Hypatia tells her son. "You have to stop doing impossible things, José. It's annoying to others. It's time to grow up."

"Why? Most grown-ups are boring. They're nothing more than deteriorated children."

Before the mother-son argument is settled, they are at Ginnie's apartment building. As though squatting to kiss the ground, Ginnie leans too far forward and tumbles into a snowbank. Hypatia and José pull on her arms to extricate her. All three laugh like silly teenagers. Only one of them has the actual excuse of being sixteen-years-old.

Hypatia and Ginnie plop down on her overstuffed sofa. They doze off immediately and commence a snoring duet. José raids Ginnie's refrigerator, leaving only crumbs and tidbits.

Hypatia and José return to Red Willow early Sunday morning. She has not quite recovered from getting scorched by the *Lantern Fuel* cocktails. She vows never to let Ginnie order drinks again and decides that all the strange goings-on at The Ornery Burro resulted from the overpriced Russian vodka they imbibed.

Hypatia takes aspirin and lies down for a nap. Father and son attend mass at St. Monica's and then drive to the Veterans' Cemetery in Six's old turquoise pickup.

They stand at the snow-covered plot with the simple white wood cross. They put their arms around one another.

"I had a dream about Tio Antonio on Thanksgiving, Papa."

"Me, too. It was his deathday. It has been one year. He said he'd visit again on his birthday in the spring to see how we're doing. I miss him more than my heart can bear."

"He will be OK, Papa. I'm pretty sure we'll see Tio Antonio up in heaven," the boy says, drying his eyes on his jacket sleeve

"Yes, I hope so, son. But he's got a lot of work ahead of him to make up for his terrible mistake."

They climb back into the pickup and Six turns up the heater.

⟫●⟪

The Monday after Thanksgiving, Hypatia takes the Greyhound bus down to Santa Fe to borrows Ginnie's sun-bleached Plymouth for the drive to Flagstaff for her interview. She drives alone. Ginnie will be in her jewelry shop every day until Christmas and will walk to her shop. José has school and Six needs his truck for work. The Mila-Grow Nursery & Greenhouse will be getting very busy with Christmas trees and wreaths.

When Six comes home after work, he smells grandma's soup. José is busy at the stove. The teenager is not always so conscientious.

"Papa. Papa," he says, nearly jumping up and down with excitement.

"Pump some water for me," Six tells his son at the kitchen sink.

"You're not listening," the teenager scolds.

"Go easy, José. I'm not taking a bath, just washing my hands. That carburetor is getting touchy again," Six says, reaching for the cake of soap.

"Something really funny happened at school today. You know my friends Bonkers and the others?"

"No, I don't, José. You never introduced me to them."

"Well, this little package fell out of my pocket. It looked just like maryjane, but it wasn't mine. Honest, Papa," José tells him, handing him the towel.

"My friends grabbed it from me..."

"Some friends," Six remarks, drying his hands and taking off his blanket-lined jean jacket.

"So they cut class and smoked it behind school," José says, interrupting his narrative with laughter.

"And?" Six inquires, dumping the loaf of spicy bread from its pan onto the cutting board beside the sink. He cuts four thick slices.

"Now my friends smell so bad they can't even stand one another. They can't wash the smell off, either. Water makes the stink stronger. They smell worse than the chicken farm over near Española."

"That's pretty bad," Six says.

"You did it. You put that plant in my pocket, didn't you? Be honest, Papa."

"I always tell the truth as I understand it, son. But keep in mind the truth is as stretchy as bread dough and it can be baked into all sorts of shapes. The *stinkwort* came from Tio Nicolás."

"I really didn't like my friends. Now I don't have to tell them that. Nobody can stand them," José laughs.

As he holds the empty bowls, his father ladles the soup his grandma taught him how to make. The teenager is still not old enough for the mushrooms, but he is allowed the broth.

They stand at the kitchen table. It is Six's day to say grace.

"Thank you, Great Spirit, for the food we have to eat and for the lessons you have taught us today. Special blessings for José and safe travels for his mother."

Father and son smile at each other and sit down to their

supper. José slathers his bread with butter and slides the crock across to his father.

———————◦◦◦———————

Hypatia returns from Flagstaff on Saturday. She is optimistic about her interview. In the evening, she receives a telegram from the University of Cambridge offering her the position she prefers. Six and José pretend they didn't know. Hypatia is elated, and unable to eat another bite. Her son and his father are no longer hungry, either, knowing how rarely they will see her.

On Sunday, Six and José drive Hypatia to the train station in Santa Fe. José rides with his mother in Ginnie's beater which she must now return to her friend. The teenager and his mother are unable to keep their conversations going. Six rides alone in the turquoise pickup, talking to himself, bracing himself for another teary good-bye. He does not want to break down in front of Hypatia.

After dropping the old Plymouth off at Ginnie's shop, Hypatia and José pile into the pickup, the long-legged teenager sitting between his parents. They drive to the train station trying to make happy small talk. Then they lapse into silence.

It takes both father and son to carry all Hypatia's luggage except for the little case with her "overnight things." The porter, in his red and black and gold uniform, the colors of the Santa Fe Chief, points to a wooden luggage cart. Hypatia shows her ticket and the porter fills out tags for the suitcases. He smiles with a wide ivory grin that contrasts with his deep brown skin.

"I'd better hurry," Hypatia says, "before I start crying."

"Oh, Mama," José says, hugging her.

Six latches onto her other side, giving her a squeeze and a salty kiss. They separate reluctantly. José hands his mother an envelope she immediately begins to tear open.

"Mama, read what it says on the envelope," José tells her.

"*Do not open until...*" she reads. "In twenty years? I couldn't possibly wait that long. Ask your father."

"I don't think she could wait twenty minutes, José. She'd read it before the train left Santa Fe. Why don't you give it to me for safekeeping, Hypatia?"

Hypatia hands the envelope to Six and turns quickly away. Father and son stand at the entrance to the enormous waiting room looking lost. Six is about to follow her inside when José grabs his father's jacket sleeve.

"I can't take another good-bye, Papa. Can we please go home?"

"You're right, José. She hopes to make it back in the summer. Still, it will be a long time to miss her."

They return to the unlocked pickup. Six holds José's letter up, making a show of putting it into the breast pocket of his jacket.

"That letter is for mama. Please don't ever open it, Papa."

"I don't have to, son. I mean... No, I won't."

"You read it, Papa. Damn it," he shouts, pounding the dashboard with his fist. "Don't I get to have anything private from you?"

"Yes, you do, José. I didn't mean to read it. But that letter was so charged, the words leapt into my fingers and popped into my mind. It's a beautiful letter."

"Tio Nicolás helped me with it last week after school."

Six starts the engine.

"So your mama's really gonna win the Nobel Prize? And become a famous astronomer like her namesake. What's a namesake, José?"

"Someone with the same name. The first Hypatia was an astronomer at the Library of Alexandria in Fourth Century Egypt."

Six backs up and heads across the parking lot, stopping at the entrance to the road.

"You're a good kid, José. And a smart kid. So then you also know you won't be going to live with Uncle Nicolás until the end of school."

"How would I know what you and mama discuss in private?"

Six places his hand on José's shoulder and gives him a firm squeeze.

"I've known for a while you can listen through walls. I didn't think you'd miss the conversations your mama and I had during her visit."

"Thank you for letting me stay until summer, Papa."

"There's one condition. You gotta get yourself some new friends that don't stink."

José nearly chokes with laughter. Six turns onto the highway and thinks about what father and son will make for their supper.

About the Author

Brian Allan Skinner has written and published more than 120 short stories which have appeared in small press and literary magazines, as well as anthologies, in the United States, Canada, and Ireland.

He is a former poetry and non-fiction reviewer for *Kirkus Reviews* and a production artist for *Scientific American Newsletters* in New York City.

In 2015, Brian moved to Taos, New Mexico, which he first visited with his grandmother on a cross-country train trip aboard the Santa Fe Chief in 1960. He quickly settled into the thriving artistic and literary communities of Taos where he draws sustenance and inspiration from his many artist and writer friends.

www.ingramcontent.com/pod-product-compliance
Lightning Source LLC
Chambersburg PA
CBHW070113260626

47160CB00004B/1441